Born in 1958, Michael Cannon left school at 17, to become variously employed as an engineer, civil servant and worker at the Sullum Voe Oil Terminal in the Shetlands, before returning to full-time education. He presently lives and works in Glasgow. His stories have appeared in the anthologies of Scottish short fiction: *I Can Sing, Dance, Rollerskate* and *A Roomful of Birds*. *The Borough* is his first novel.

The Borough

MICHAEL CANNON

Library of Congress Catalog Card Number: 94-67715

A complete catalogue record for this book can be obtained from the British Library on request

The right of Michael Cannon to be identified as the author of this work has been asserted by him in accordance with the Copyright, Designs and Patents Act 1988

First published in 1995 by
Serpent's Tail, 4 Blackstock Mews, London N4, and
401 West Broadway #1, New York, NY 10012

Set in 10pt Plantin by Servis Filmsetting Ltd, Manchester
Printed in Great Britain by Cox & Wyman Ltd, Reading, Berkshire

The Borough

1

THE FIRST THING anyone who's anyone finds out when they come to the Borough is that the sub-postmaster's wife fakes it. "Take me! For fuck's sake take me!" she shouts, they say. So frenzied are her histrionics he is obliged to wear two pullovers in bed, it is alleged, to protect his back as she scratches and writhes with the frenzy of a corybant. How everyone knows this, no one knows. It is an uncorroborated piece of malicious gossip which has found its way into local folklore. Produced at nights-out and embellished upon, like a pearl it has grown by accretion, layer upon layer, until the absurdity of the Frew's sexual antics have become the canon of Borough humour. Such is the sad machismo of this enclave.

Go into that musty Post Office any day of the week, take a look at the shy man who peers out behind his guichet and suffers the hesitations of his customers with patience, and still you have not appreciated the cruel humour of the shared joke to its full extent. Simon Frew is shambling towards middle age. By all the rules of popular fiction his wife should be a sloe-eyed woman in her sexual prime, who eats twice as much as he does, provocatively sucks asparagus tips and licks dollups of mayonnaise from her fingers with erotic relish. A home bird and a cocotte, a book worm and a voluptuary: these combinations would corroborate the joke. But Elsbeth Frew has taken a house as far from the Borough main street as property values allow, and ignores the grubbing poor from which she emerged by contriving an air of glacial preoccupation. When she descends to shop she adopts the attitude of a bishop *in partibus*. She has one abiding Presbyterian obsession: a morbid fear that somewhere, someone is having a good time. His shy amiability and her Victorian prudery lend the joke of their coupling its perennial humour.

I was idling at the Lament bar when she strutted past. Through the windows of frosted Victorian glass we could see her blurred outline, dowdily buttoned to the throat against the wind and concupiscence. I think she thought sin something circumambient which inhabited the air between bodies, infecting the unwary – especially men.

"There she goes," said Tom. "May God bless her and all who sail in her." Several laughed. I didn't get the joke.

"Semen," David explained.

I ordered three more drinks, lager that slopped against the bar and was wiped by the aproned barman. It was the curious interim beyond afternoon and not yet evening, a lull the Piper's Lament conveniently filled for many. The Borough is full of such haunts.

"Why doesn't that joke age? Why does no one else seem to find it cruel?"

They turned to me. "You weren't born here. You're a foreigner. You'll always be a foreigner, even if you stay here for the next twenty years and die standing at this bar."

That was the extent of their explanation.

We could make out the silhouette of Simon's progress window by window till he reached the door. The barman, by similar clairvoyance, handed us another lager. Tom laid down the money. When he came in Simon looked slowly round and walked towards us. Tom handed him the drink which he took automatically. It was the most natural transaction I've seen. He took the first sip and winced, glanced quickly at us and then studied the floor.

"Stamps," he said quietly, dabbing his tongue, and took another sip. Perhaps he even knew he was a stock joke. In the Borough all know one another so well each typifies something.

"Why don't you get Elsbeth to do some licking with that big red tongue of hers?" David said.

They leaned towards one another in perfect equilibrium. They had been born here.

2

IT IS ONEROUS to be the repository of too many secrets. Perhaps there is something in my appearance which inspires trust. I do not desire these confidences. Feigned hostility had not deterred them. And I hear things. I hear the casual cruelty of a chance remark. I hear the indiscreet admissions of children at play. And I hear Irene in the small hours who doesn't hear me. She is talking to no one, to her sleeping baby, to herself.

She says the earth's heating up. It's to do with depletion of the atmosphere. She says the sunlight's getting through and the earth's heating. The polar caps will melt and half the Borough will be under water. And the universe is cooling. She says it's called entropy. She says she read about it in a magazine at the dentist. They're chopping down trees to make newspapers so we can read about it. No more oxygen. So either we'll drown, or burn, or suffocate. But she says she can take it. Eventually the sun's going to expand, then implode – and take us with it. No more picture postcards. She says she can take that. She says she's a slugger. She can take anything cosmic. She can take the lack of money and the cheaper cuts of meat. She can tolerate the paper in her shoe. She's hardy. She can take the doing without and even his squandering his money at the bar. As long as she gets for her kids. She can take his drunkenness and his tempers and his clumsy caresses. She'll bounce back. What she can't take is his looking at her in cold sobriety and not caring.

3

I CAME HERE by accident. It took me a while to realise that the Borough was unique, even for Glasgow. It is poor, and yet it lives cheek-by-jowl with the wealthier districts which ring the University precincts. This is a strange symbiosis. The University surmounts the hill, its Gothic pile silhouetted by day and floodlit by night. The spire is a landmark for miles. Many of the academics live within walking distance. Small mews flats off cobbled lanes now fetch exorbitant prices. People with more money than sense pay for the prestige of living where a horse was once stalled. This is the city's Bohemia. Across the Kelvin immense town houses, built for the tobacco barons when Glasgow was still the second city of the empire, have been converted into student residences.

On Friday afternoons, and only by appointment, the Bedellus will take you up the tower. A grudging old man with angina, he welcomes neither the climb nor the sudden chill at the top. He will not budge an inch unless the group reaches its full complement. The staircase is a tight spiral spattered with pigeon droppings. But the view is worth the climb.

You can look at the surrounding hills. You can look at the meandering Kelvin. You can look at the manicured quads. And you can look down the hill towards the Borough. The transition is less obvious than it used to be. The first time I made the trip down the hill I noticed the deteriorating pavements which broke my stride. The small tended stretches of grass outside tenement blocks became trampled, muddy, littered with detritus and then disappeared completely. The plethora of delicatessens petered out into frugal licensed grocers and off-sales with merchandise behind bars. *Fromage de chèvre* gave way to coloured cheddar. Accents changed. Conversations were circumscribed by more pragmatic considerations than those addressed up the hill. There was, and still is, a noticeable lack of bookshops.

For years before I arrived the Borough workforce had been almost totally monopolised by the shipbuilding industry. The yards threw open their gates and the school leavers entered in droves to become platers, welders, fitters and all the kinds of tradesmen necessary to build ships. Streets thronged at the change-over in shifts. Bars enjoyed frantic trade till the crowds subsided. Hulks grew in the dry dock. Early winter evenings the blue flash of the arc welders could be seen in the half dark till the shift finished. Launches were a jamboree with streets and doors bedizened for the occasion. And when the decline in heavy industry cut deepest the Borough fell silent. Redundant men watched television while their self-esteem atrophied. Small retailers, dependent on workforce trade, closed doors and boarded their windows. Rusting cranes stood like some social hieroglyph – an indictment and a reminder.

My arrival coincided with a resurgence in civic pride. This was fortuitous. I'm not making any claims. Besides which, the worst of the recession had passed. The Borough had passed its nadir. Not all those who took redundancy frittered their compensation. Some ventures went to the wall, some small entrepreneurs emerged. Others formed a workers' cooperative. Business brought business and engendered more. Local Authority projects to upgrade existing accommodation generated money spent locally. A multitude of bedsits sprang up inhabited by students: Bohemia condescended to slope down the hill. A steady influx of Asians and others established colonies within a colony, and the staple High Street diet of fish and chips extended to Tagliatelle Caruso, Chicken Korma and Egg Foo Yung. The bars, which had never emptied in the darkest of recessions, remained full.

Some of the older inhabitants might stand, glass in hand, and deplore the loss of bygone days and a decent homogeneity, but the curious thing is that, so I'm told, throughout its transformation, the Borough never lost its identity. Everything appears to have been assimilated – except me. Passions run close to the skin here, both violent and humane. The chicken vol-au-vent and gingham table cloths haven't changed that.

4

PETER IS FISHING in the Clyde. Peter is an optimist. Having nothing better to do, I sat beside him. It was getting on for evening. The sky was a flaming crescent.

"Do you think Irene likes me?" he asked.

"You obviously do."

He sat watching the line hanging motionless in the limpid water before he spoke again.

"Can I tell you something?"

"Is it private?"

"Yes."

"Keep it to yourself," I said. "I'm up to here with other people's secrets."

"Whose?"

"If I told you would you still want to tell me your secret?"

"Why not?"

"Because if I'm prepared to volunteer other people's confidences at your say so, what guarantee do you have that I wouldn't do the same with yours?"

"I never thought of that."

"Yes you did. You're just like everyone else. You think there's no point in having a secret unless you tell someone else that it exists. And it's a small step from telling that it exists to what it is."

"Really?" It was a feeble attempt at incredulity.

"And if you tell it to me it'll save you the trouble of peddling it round yourself."

"Fuck off!"

"There's nothing very private about you, Peter."

A silence endured which he tried hard to maintain. It was difficult not to laugh.

"I've a friend . . ." he began. That was enough. I once went with him to the Urology clinic to lend moral support when he thought he had a dose of the clap. He came back out to the waiting room with a tropical blush. It seems he saw the consultant and said he once knew a man who thought he'd picked up something from a toilet pan. The doctor told him to take down his trousers or get out and not waste both their times. I laughed at that as I laughed at this disingenuous opening.

"I'm sorry. No, really. You've a friend . . ."

He refused to continue.

"What age are you?"

"Twenty-five. Why?"

"What age is she?"

"Twenty-eight."

"Is that all?"

"You think she looks older."

"No, not looks older. I just assumed she was older. It's a matter of attitude and the way she acts."

"What kind of attitude do you suppose you'd have with two kids and an old man like hers drinking half the house-keeping?"

"Yes. You're right. And you'll take her away from all that?"

"Too right. Some figure. Some of these young mothers . . ." He tailed off in wistful anticipation. "Ever spectated at the baths near the kids' pool?"

"No."

"Boring bastard."

He resumed his vigil, hunched over the stationary line.

5

WHAT AGE AM I? I suppose I am a certain age. Many people use the expression "a certain age" precisely because they do not want to reveal exactly what age they are. A certain age is the age at which people prefer to deal in approximations. And a certain age varies from person to person depending on their sensitivity with regard to their years.

I am not in the least sensitive in this area. If I was candid about my years I would not be believed. I cannot, in all honesty, say I look my age. I do not look any age. This indeterminism has its advantages. I am welcome in all kinds of company: I can go fishing with Peter, I have played hopscotch on the pavements with the primary children and pretended to smoke cigarettes with Mr Paterson, the Borough Methuselah, laid up with lumbago in his decrepit flat, wheezing up tarry phlegm, the ubiquitous fag end clutched between fingers the colour of saffron with strata of nicotine. His first name disappeared in the mists of antiquity: out of reverence no one has used it since. But his interview with me, and mine with the children, have nothing to do with age condescending to frivolity. Although they do not have my privileged access, I talk with people as equals or I do not talk to them at all. Fortunately there are few this approach excludes me from, and they are not worth the knowing anyway.

6

DANIEL SENSES his mother's agitation and will not sleep. His restlessness will wake the baby he shares the room with. She carries him through to the lounge and props him in front of the television in his pyjamas, returning with the blanket which she wraps around him. She sits across the room in a chair beside the coffee table on which the anglepoise is perched. Occasionally her eyes flick from the book in front of her to the child's face. His head is nodding till the novelty of the nine o'clock news alerts him. He is four years old and cannot remember having seen nine o'clock before. By the time the main features have elapsed he is again torpid, nodding off at the commentator's monologue.

She picks him up without resistance. Settling him to her satisfaction she automatically checks the baby before returning to the lounge. Aside from the anglepoise, the only other light comes from the television screen. She stands in the centre of the room, temporarily at a loss, gazing blankly. The monologue passes her, the grey square of light doubly reflected in her retinas. No comprehension is registered. Summoning herself, she turns off the television, sits down in her chair and hoists the book before her face again. Scanning from side to side she reads the same paragraph twice without noticing.

Ten o'clock and she can feel the pulse in her neck. She has been looking sightlessly at the same page for some time. It is Friday: McCullen has been given his wages. The meal which he did not present himself for is sandwiched between two plates and placed in the fridge. Everything in the flat has been placed, since she spent the past two hours doing superfluous housework, dusting and replacing ornaments with unnecessary precision.

At each noise in the stairwell she stands with the front door slightly ajar and listens. She has commuted six times between lounge and hallway to hear the ordinary traffic of the other tenants. Lately she has begun to perceive herself as the archetype her mother spoke of with sympathy and guarded disparagement: the beaten wife. Except that he never hits her.

There is an erratic tread on the stairway, slow and unpredictably halting. It can only be him. She leaves the front door off the latch lest the rattle of his keys wake the children, and returns to the pretence of her book. At finding no resistance to his key he pushes the door wide, banging it against the jamb, then makes an elaborate show of closing it quietly. Her ears are cocked: the pause is excruciating. He discards his coat and walks towards the light.

"Expecting someone?"

"I left the door . . ."

"Come into my parlour," he interrupts. "Kids?"

"Asleep."

He stands rocking in front of the fire, supporting himself with one hand on the mantelpiece.

"Dinner?"

"In the fridge between plates."

He turns his back and lurches towards the kitchen, an alcove off the lounge separated by an entrance over which the factor has nailed a piece of plywood with hanging vinyl fronds. He pushes these aside and entangles his arm. She can see his face wanly lit by the interior light as he pulls open the fridge. He disentangles himself with a shrug and returns, sitting in the same space the boy had occupied two hours previously. Facing her he prises off the upper plate.

"Salad!" He scavenges with his fingers. "Where did you get this meat?"

"From a tin."

"What tin?"

"It came in the hamper my mother sent us at Christmas."

"Oh – *your* mother."

She refuses to be drawn. He eats the meat, gathers together the remainder and throws it on the fire. She can hear the slices of tomato hiss as they contact the hot embers. She says nothing.

"Rabbit food." He stands and moves towards the toilet. She can hear him pat either wall as he sways along the narrow hall. The toilet door closes noisily behind him. From downstairs she can hear the preparatory drum roll, hastily turned off, as "God Save the Queen" closes down the airway with quotidian pomp. He comes back and lights a cigarette, standing against the fireplace. Taking the pay envelope from his hip pocket he makes elaborate show of placing it beneath the clock. She maintains her pretence of reading, hoping sufficient remains to see them through the week.

"Saw a woman in the pub. Girl really. Your age. I think she was at school with you."

She looks up.

"What was her name?"

"Dunno. Sheila . . . Shona?"

"Shona Murray?"

He snaps his fingers. "The very one. I never remembered her as much. Always seemed a bit, a bit . . . unprepossessing." He is startled by his own eloquence, at this pleasantly alien word trespassing on his vocabulary. "Yes, unprepossessing. Not to say plain. But she stood there tonight. Done something to her hair too. Looked younger. Takes care of herself. Y'know?"

He waits. She pretends to be abstracted.

"Nice figure too. I never noticed before. Keeps looking across. Seems like she's giving me the glad eye. I don't know who she was with but I'm sure her cunt wanted a word with me."

He has never spoken so blatantly before. She is on the verge of tears, puts down her book and lifts her fingers to her temples.

"Headache? Anyway, she came over and had a word. I bought her a drink. She was going to buy me one back but I told her I had to come home to . . ." he makes an expansive gesture "domestic bliss . . . I wonder if her clitoris tastes like an anchovy the way yours used to."

He takes a final draw on his cigarette, incinerating the remaining tobacco, throws the end in the fire and exhales a goodnight in her direction. She waits, crying silently till there is no noise from the bedroom. She goes to the clock, removes the envelope and counts the remaining notes. It is not as bad as she feared. She replaces the envelope where she found it, secreting her purse at the bottom of her bag. She goes to the bathroom and prepares herself as noiselessly as possible. The orbits of her eyes have adopted a permanent smudge. With a final check on the children she enters the bedroom. The curtains are open, the angle of his shoulder visible above the duvet from the pale lamplight shining in.

What has happened? This is not just a cooling off. All would be simple but for the simple fact that she is still in love. For the sake of sanity she can only think of his words as the unfounded raving of a deluded man ranting in his cups, lashing out in misguided self-resentment at the things for which he most cares. She has seen as much before with those ugly pavement brawls after closing. A wave of compassion such as she daily lavishes upon her children wells up in her. Sliding in beside him she covers his bare shoulder with the duvet.

"Not tonight, Josephine," he says, without opening his eyes.

7

I WAS STANDING talking beside one of the alcoves when I saw McCullen approach Shona out of the corner of my eye. The exchange was beyond earshot. Receiving an obvious rebuff he finished off the dregs and ambled out. I continued my conversation with Kate. She was talking about habits. Like most others, the pub burst with armchair psychologists: people watching people watching people.

"I've a friend . . ." she began.

"So has Peter."

He'd been standing on the periphery of the group, nurturing a drink and looking for a pretext to interrupt the conversation. I've heard him refer to Kate in the past as "pneumatic", but then his stock of adjectives is not large and he has referred to most women in the same way. On hearing his name he seized the opportunity. I ignored Kate's imploring look and followed McCullen out.

His attitude of late has been ominous. There is a contained violence in his brooding that deters even his acquaintances. I do not know if someone like McCullen could claim friends. I was at the close entrance when I heard his front door shut. I walked quietly to the half-landing and stood for perhaps twenty minutes. There was no sound of raised voices. Perhaps, despite my fear, I even wanted to intercede.

I didn't go back to the bar; I turned my steps towards my lodgings.

8

THE BABY WAKES around six. Irene is instantaneously conscious at the first sound. What sleep she gets these days is intermittent and brittle. Slipping on her housecoat she closes the door behind her and hurries through. McCullen is still in a stupor. Picking the baby up Irene deftly quietens her.

On previous Saturdays she has taken the baby through, settled her on the bed between them. Now, suddenly, she bridles at the prospect of going back in there with him. Nor does she want Elizabeth near her father this morning. Daniel's bed is an adult's, hers before she was married. Shaking him gingerly she urges the boy to move across. He is docile and shifts almost without waking. She lies beside him, on her back, the baby resting on her chest and stomach. She drifts off.

9

SATURDAY: THE WEEKLY reprieve. For no reason other than the fact that I had not done so for some time, I set off in high spirits for the Museum and Art Gallery. This is a curious miscellany, a stone's throw from the Borough. Sam, the moth-eaten Bengal tiger who died in the Calderpark Zoo in 1964, vies with fossils, samurai swords, Charles Rennie Mackintosh interiors and Cézanne for the privilege. I met Kate on the way.

"Coming?"

"Where?"

"Art Gallery."

"I'll get you part of the way. Have they still got the Tyrannosaurus?"

"And the Salvador Dali."

"It's some organ."

"What?"

"Big organ. Wind pipes and everything. They give evening recitals in the winter."

"Yes."

"Have they still got the bees?"

"They've got those bees crucified on to card with a big pin, beside the butterflies and all the other insects."

"No, not those bees. They used to have a hive in cross-section set into a glass panel on the wall and you could see them making honey."

"Not that I'm aware."

"And the giraffe with the ripped legs?"

Another feed line. I refused to encourage her but she needed no prompting.

"They bent it down towards the false water-hole they'd painted. Its legs burst and the stuffing poured out. So they sewed them up. But you can still see the splits."

"Really. I usually go for the paintings."

"All I remember about that place is the school trips: the squeaking parquet floors and janitors telling us to shut up." She paused for a minute, the reminiscence of juvenile nostalgia leading to a topic I'd hoped to avoid. "By the way, thanks for abandoning me with the boy last night."

"He's the same age you are."

"He's clueless. He's about as subtle as the stuffed tiger

they've got in there, you know the one who died in the Calderpark Zoo in 1964."

"Sam."

"Yes, Sam."

"What did he say?"

"What do all drunks say? He started off about the cosmos and worked his way down to a proposition."

"There's some novelty in the approach, even if the end result is always the same."

"You're not subjected to it."

"What did you say?"

"I thought you had a reputation for being clever?" She stopped. "Anyway, this is me."

Ten minutes previously I'd have been happy enjoying a solitary day with the immortals. Now I wanted her company.

"Come see the Degas."

"Come with me and buy beetroot."

I stood indecisively. Then she said: "You'd sooner look at pictures of fruit than fruit."

It stung me. She was right. And I wasn't getting any better.

10

ELIZABETH WILL SLEEP no longer than nine. Irene dresses, sees to the children, prepares breakfast. McCullen, crapulous, ignores the mug of tea left for him on the bureau.

Giving him another twenty minutes while she feeds the

children and herself, Irene takes another mug through and coaxes him awake. She will not leave them alone in the house with him still asleep, nor does she want to take them with her. Shopping with kids in tow is arduous enough during the week. As he lumbers to the toilet she removes the envelope from under the clock, does a quick calculation and takes as little as will reasonably cover the immediate expense. The rest, if husbanded, will see them to the end of the week.

He is sitting in the only reasonable chair left, rolling cigarettes and watching television by the time she leaves. The children are playing. The morning is fresh. Unencumbered, she resumes the jaunty manner his presence now dispels. She walks in the sunshine, calling at the fruit stalls first, examining the textures as she selects. She only uses supermarkets as a last resort. She stops outside the fishmonger, exhibiting an almost childish awe at the scaled bodies shining on the slab. An inadvertent meeting with Shona causes embarrassment on either side. By the other girl's rising colour Irene knows that there must have been some exchange the previous evening. They smile without looking at one another and part.

Her other meetings are pleasant interludes.

A sudden shower finds her running for shelter. The park café is near. These days coffee is an extravagance, but the rain and the proximity of the place seem too fortuitous to pass up. The place is staffed by students supplementing their grants. Business is sufficiently slack to allow the waitress to loiter, chatting. Fifteen minutes later Irene is out again. Another hour finds her climbing the stair laden down and pleasantly flushed. It does not take much to make her happy. She is thinking: "perhaps tonight, with a family meal . . ."

indisposed towards his attentions and accepted his offer prior to its being made. The banns were published before he drew breath and within three months she had wed, bedded and installed him in a Glasgow tenement five minutes off the Trongate. It was a harsh transition for this affably lackadaisical man to find himself, within a year, a prospective father lugging ingots of pig iron round the Dixon Blazes at sixpence on the ton. It didn't line his pockets but it compressed his spine. He gave his employer twenty good years and an inch and a half in height.

She was brought to confinement and their first was born, Sandra, apple of her father's eye, with the same winning manner and effortless charm. The flat shrank, the pulley nightly festooned with drying nappies. Elsbeth was ushered two years later into a two-room-and-kitchen which could barely accommodate the bric-a-brac of a spinster.

There was no classical symmetry to Sandra's features, but she enjoyed rude animal health and a beauty which shone with her raw vigour. Of Elsbeth it would be kind to use McCullen's word "unprepossessing". It was an obvious disparity, which she learned early and had daily to endure. She grew to dread the tacit comparisons of family reunions. Her mother felt for the child, and made what redress she could to compensate for the natural bias towards the obvious favourite. Elsbeth was brought up with the repeated maxim that beauty is in the eye of the beholder. True as this might be, she was astute enough to realise that this is the usual argument which the ugly, or their comforters, have recourse to. And besides, aesthetic subjectivity is small comfort when the consensus of beholders normally agrees on what is desirable to look at and what is not. Sandra knew this by instinct and milked what advantage it wrought. Elsbeth was to come to know this and it is a pity, inheriting as much from her mother as she did, that she did not inherit the generosity of spirit to mitigate her bitterness.

The father was Laodicean in matters of religion, as affably vague towards God as he was towards everyone else. The mother sent the girls to Sunday school without attending a service herself, and on Christmas Eve hauled them up to the Cathedral for watch-night service. Sandra imbibed the rudiments of the Protestant faith which served her as a touchstone. When Elsbeth got her hands on the Bible there was no looking back.

She became one of those people who scour the good book looking for quotations to substantiate their prejudices, jettisoning the rest as contradictory or irrelevant. Aside from the Song of Songs, she preferred the Old Testament to the New, the proscriptions of the Commandments to the prescriptions of the Sermon on the Mount. Faith became a way of forbidding things.

An unhealthy sense of propriety manifested itself at an early age. It is difficult to cultivate modesty in a two-room-and-kitchen when the father bathes nightly in a galvanised zinc tub before the fire. When Elsbeth enrolled at secretarial college, Sandra chose a suitor and their father bankrupted the family, mobilising their scant means for the trousseau of his favourite daughter. She left for a car salesman and the bliss of a terraced house in Huddersfield. In her absence the two-room expanded and cooled.

A room of one's own at eighteen. And just when she was re-arranging the bibelots, her mother drew her aside and announced the move. The cosmopolitan life was proving too much after a twenty-year experiment, what with the hurly-burly of Sauchiehall Street and her father's back, they were returning to Ayrshire. She was invited to join them. But an Ayrshire village was where couples settled or people retired to. She could commute, but self-imposed exile at eighteen was tantamount to acceptance of premature spinsterhood. And she had more spirit than that. So she politely declined and began to read the accommodation lists in the *Glasgow Evening News*. Saturday afternoon found her viewing with intention to rent. She had two mental provisos: the place should be clean and free from papists. Simon Frew was shuffling towards the Underground when a curious creature, with what looked like a large library book under her arm, hove into sight.

12

"LEAVE THE BASTARD. Just leave him."

Irene looked into her face. It is easy to speak with conviction when you are remote from the consequences. Carol is her age and unattached. She is insulated from the hardships Irene endures. A regular income and her own place three flights above the street give her the luxury of impartiality.

"Let him come home and see no meal. Let the bastard learn to cook. Up and leave him."

"I'm twenty-eight. I've two children. I'll not land them on my parents."

"Come to mine."

The offer is no less sincere for being instantaneous. They have grown up together. Occasionally Irene envies Carol: her independence, her time, her foreign holidays. But only occasionally. There is a price paid for children, and for childlessness. Carol is a romantic itinerant. A rapid turnover of men friends at her age, in the Borough, adds up to promiscuity in public opinion. She is similarly rootless in work. She has shunted from retail to secretarial work to the lower echelons of the civil service in as many years. Now she is filling a gap between employments as a waitress. As long as income exceeds immediate outlay she will survive. It is a short-term equilibrium. Sometimes Irene pities her for the men she has slept with and the situations vacated. She has run the gamut before thirty.

"You've no room."

"Is the sofa yours or his?"

"Mine." The ease with which this comes out shocks her. Has she already compiled some unconscious inventory?

"Is it a sofa-bed?"

"Yes."

"There's the other room."

Irene, the more realistic of the two, can see the consequences: the continual rota of children's drying clothes, the bathroom monopolised while Carol prepares for work, the difficult intimacy with her men with a family through the wall.

"Guests and fish, like the man said, stink after three days. I wouldn't like it to cloud things between us."

"The offer's there."

"Thanks. Even if I don't take you up on it. The option alone is a comfort." She takes Carol's hand. "Who are you seeing just now?"

"You."

"Not right now – lately?"

"A lecturer. A historian. Or as he says, an historian. Except he leaves out the 'h'. In other circumstances he'd consider that vulgar. 'Vulgar' is another one of his words."

"And is he vulgar?"

"Perish the thought. He talks about conjoining and sexual congress. 'Call it what you want' I told him, the first time, 'I'm in the mood for a shag'."

"Carol!"

"He said a rose by any other name."

"Is he married?"

"He says he's divorced."

13

"EXCUSE ME," SAID Elsbeth, nineteen years ago, "is this Kinkarth Street?"

"No. That's Kinkarth Street. Are you looking for the library?"

"No."

"Because it's on Kinkarth Street."

"As the library is not the object of my attention, its absence will not incommode me in the slightest." Like her prudery at her father's nightly nakedness, her manner of speech was an over-reaction to the mangled syntax of her home. She was ashamed.

"It's just . . ."

"Yes?"

"What's the book?"

"It's *the* book."

"It looks big."

"It's a *very* big book. It's *the* biggest book ever written."

"Who wrote it?"

Hesitantly, "Several people."

"A sort of collection."

"Y . . . es."

Having exhausted the topic of conversation he stood embarrassed, and leaned in the direction he intended to go. With a guarded smile directed at the ground, and the sky, and anywhere but her, he prepared to move off.

"Do you know where sixteen is?"

"Yes. There."

"Which one?"

"Middle."

"There are eight in the terrace."

"Really? I've lived there all my life and never noticed."

"Can you take me?"

Hands in pockets, eyes intent on the ground, colour in either cheek, he began walking towards number sixteen. She walked just behind. It was the only time they ever travelled in this formation.

"Which floor?"

"Second."

He had come this far. What was the decent thing to do? It was the first time he had kept company beside a girl for more than five minutes since the school playground. As he trudged up the stairs he realised the absence of the sound of heels in his wake. Stopping on the landing he glanced at her brogues, utilitarian and entirely without charm. Without explaining he continued.

On the second floor he indicated the wrong door. Reading the name opposite she rang the bell. An elderly woman appeared, smiled benignly at the mystified Simon and gestured them in.

The place was scrupulous. Elsbeth quickly reconnoitred, looking for the tell-tale artefacts. Having discussed terms over tea she braced herself.

"You're not . . . papists?"

"I wouldn't have the Whore of Babylon over the threshold," said the present to the future Mrs Frew.

Simon ate his cake in silence.

14

"DR HENRY CARR M.A. D.PHIL," read his cards, "Historian". Not "history lecturer" or "mere reciter of facts". "The age which knows nothing of history, knows nothing of the age in which . . . it . . . lives" he says, gamely misquoting Wilde to generations. "History is a continuum" is another of his favourites "and we are merely its latest increment". He has a stock of such sonorous phrases which mean absolutely nothing. And he has no idea of the year in which he lives. Years ago he obtained security of tenure and irrevocably drafted his lecture notes the following day: tissues of other people's opinions loosely strung together by his inferior prose. These he had the departmental secretary type up, and at each autumn intake runs off innumerable copies which he circulates among his students, retiring in the knowledge that he has done his bit. He fights changes in the curriculum tooth and nail.

It is an unfortunate coincidence, not all of his making, to be a historian and to be called Carr without the privilege of being able to claim kinship with his illustrious namesake. Henry struggles against a feeling of innate inferiority by a number of means. He introduces himself as "Doctor Carr". This has led to several *débâcles*: one woman in the supermarket described her pruritus in detail. He is also pompous in his turn of expression: people are never bawdy but Rabelaisian, never whimsical but Quixotic, never shrewd but Machiavellian, never cowardly but pusillanimous, never beautiful but pulchritudinous.

He has brought two of his third year female students down to the college club, signed them in with a flourish, installed them near the fireplace and put in front of each a glass of cheap, bitter Muscat. He keeps his own pewter tankard behind the bar. This he has filled with a bottle of stout, taking a seat opposite the young women.

"So what do you think?" His wave takes in the baronial hearth and the discarded newspapers. They do not seem suitably impressed to volunteer any remark, but make vague self-deprecating gestures towards one another. He decides to pursue another tack.

"What do you two read?"

"History," says Pamela.

"We're in your class," says Jane.

"Yes, of course. I meant newspapers."

"I barely get time," said Pamela, "with all those books we're recommended."

Pamela is rather pretty. As is often the case with rather pretty girls, she kept company with plain girls. She kept company with Jane, a plump girl, who steered her the way plump girls often have of steering slender ones. Henry finds Jane's company quite superfluous.

"Ah – the syllabus." He has taken to smoking a pipe. It lends, he feels, a certain dignity denied him by his height. He blows down the stem, peppering his beer with black ash. "And who compiled the syllabus? Professor Hawthorne. Are either of you studying the Russo–Japanese war?" The phrase is produced with a sonorous roll, like distant artillery.

27

"No," from Jane.

"Pity. There is a specific book, practically useless, prescribed by Professor Hawthorne. Written by whom? Professor Hawthorne. I myself published a paper . . ."

"Are you any relation to that other Carr?"

"I myself published a paper on the subject entitled 'The Sickle and the Samurai'." He gives further effect with a wave of the hand. The thread of saliva which attenuates from lip to stem glistens as he gesticulates. "Steamed halfway round the world to go down like . . ." he has noticed the foam of his beer pockmarked with ash.

"Ships," says Jane.

"Yes. Fascinating."

"Do you think it's possible," Jane asks, "to plot the frequency of questions in past papers and predict what questions will come up in the finals?"

"That depends . . ." A rank cloud has emerged from the bowl. How does one clean these things? How does Hawthorne smoke with such aplomb?

"On what?"

"On . . . the questions." He knows little of his colleagues' professional affairs and cares even less, classifying them only by the extent to which they upstage him. Two years ago a malicious rumour had been circulated within the University, intimating that for services to the department he would be installed as Regius professor. He believed it to the extent of having his chequebook changed and a brass nameplate etched, both with his new prefix, measures which he later denied.

"But surely that begs the question?"

"Which one?" he asks, not looking at her. He is looking up Pamela's skirt. Her legs disappear into a folded bell. Her thighs are charming, quite charming.

"Which papers do you think will come up, Dr Carr?" asks Pamela.

"That would be telling."

"That's why I asked. To be told."

She is moving her legs. Charming, quite charming.

"Italian reunification." His mind draws a blank. "I'd have to think of the probability." Another fumbling silence as he delves into his pockets and produces a pen knife. The blades are mentally identified as he unfolds them: for cutting quills, for removing stones from horses' hooves, for opening bottles. Where is the thing which tamps down tobacco? Perhaps he has bought the wrong knife. How does Hawthorne manage the thing?

"Do you believe in historical probability?" Jane asks.

"What?" He has found a blade whose purpose he is unable to identify.

"Do you believe in the Hegelian principle that history is governed like science, by a series of immutable laws? Or do you believe the 'Cleopatra's Nose' theory?"

"Bloody third-years," he is thinking.

"Is everything just a fortuitous concourse of atoms?" Pamela chimes in.

"That's philosophy," Jane corrects. "Existentialism – first year."

The meerschaum stem snaps in his hands. A black residue of saliva pours from the broken end over the crotch of his worsted trousers.

"Fuck!"

"Oh, you use that word too," says Pamela.

Jane downs her drink at a single swallow and nods to her companion who does likewise. He escorts them out, covering the offending stain with the palm of his hand. The janitor in the quad, towards whose Christmas he never contributed and who, in reprisal, perpetrated the rumour of Henry's specious promotion, winks at him in passing.

"Perhaps you'd like a chair?" he asks.

15

IF ANYTHING IN this continuum of mine can be located, then it was at this point in time when things began to go seriously awry with me. I fell in love with a whole family.

I met the three daughters variously, at different times, introduced to all three by a mutual friend. The fascination with the family began when I was invited out to one of their innumerable parties. Because of my wanderings I have always been poor. I have never stayed in any one place long enough to amass any money. The size and affluence of their home threw into relief my own stark quarters.

There seemed to be no particular reason why so many had gathered in their house on that occasion, but the profusion of food and their casual largesse piqued my curiosity. Aside from the three daughters, all of whom I knew, or knew of, the remainder of the guests were strange to me. With no particular family resemblance I could not pick out the mother or father in the throng, and felt uneasy at the prospect of making some gaffe in front of my hosts. I left alone and after midnight, unintroduced. It was not that kind of party. I felt sure that I had done nothing conspicuous to mark my passing. When I became attached to one of the daughters I felt ill at ease: my circumstances were obscure, I did not know how to prosecute my suit.

Mr Paton was Welsh in origin, the mother German, a curious heritage which, since the daughters were raised bilingually, lent them a certain cosmopolitan chic in their provincial setting. She had been educated at a convent school by Catholic nuns on a small island in the middle of a German lake. The cloying piety left her with a recalcitrant atheism which she passed on. No men were permitted there aside from the priests who daily rowed out to serve mass. A similar establishment on another island twenty minutes distant was populated by schoolboys. No one had the temerity to swim the gap.

Of the parents she was the more noteworthy of the two and certainly, to an outsider, presided over all household matters. Sanguine in temperament and complexion, I invariably found her in her garden during my infrequent visits of the summer months. Small, open-faced, she seemed to have passed on none of her physical characteristics to her daughters. Her two youngest had a kind of luminous delicate beauty in marked contrast to their mother who often reminded me of a happy churl. She had coined a series of family words, half-English, half-German, which she handed on to her children. To the outsider around the dinner table, the family vocabulary was half gibberish. Allied to this was the fact that the daughters, like the Brontës before them, had invented several sobriquets for each other. The impression was of a closed coterie. The manner of the mother's upbringing and the genetic accident of having only female children provided the atmosphere of the house with two of its most distinguishing characteristics: it was almost exclusively female and completely atheistic. The Patons had no need of metaphysics. She became a secondary school teacher.

The father I hardly knew at all. Clever and withdrawn,

he foisted on me, within the first twenty minutes of our first meeting, lager, *crudités*, olives, a glass of calvados and a copy of his filmgoers' companion. This he did in lieu of conversation. It took me some time to realise that this continuous traffic, with which he confronted me on the few times we met, was a kind of *cordon sanitaire*. Behind his intelligence and hospitality he was socially inept and enormously shy. I don't ever remember him volunteering to me a single remark. The few exchanges we had I initiated out of a sense of propriety to earn my keep. I don't think he ever really knew who I was: I was classed as one of the vague legion of men who had come to pay attention to one or other of his daughters. A scientist of some kind, he had founded an engineering department at a local polytechnic, whose industrial spin-offs had paid unexpected dividends. He was a totally innocuous man. I always remember him being tense, as if working under some immense pressure, his only seeming purpose to generate enough money to maintain his beautiful house and subsidise his daughters' predilections.

Katrine, the youngest, was just nineteen when I first knew her, newly matriculated at Glasgow University. Tall, slender, she wore her hair cropped short and carried herself with a schoolgirl jauntiness. She had a kind of inchoate beauty, recently emerged, whose novelty she was learning to exploit. She was astute enough to know she had two years of ingenuousness left to her, and intended to ward off the world with her father's chequebook for as long as he would tolerate. Like her sisters she was constantly importuned by men.

Rhys, the eldest, was fascinating. She never particularly liked me and never took the trouble to disguise the fact, which piqued my curiosity even further. I even felt a grudging admiration for this aspect of her brutal candour. Dark where the others were blonde, mercurial where they were placid, precocious, she somehow failed to live up to early expectations. Vegetarian and feminist, she disappeared to Oxford for three years and came back with a respectable degree in English and, like her mother, taught for a living. I saw her once during her student days when she had temporarily adopted a veneer of sophistication which she thankfully dropped. Her vegetarianism similarly lapsed. Suspecting they had a prodigy on their hands, her parents had done her the disservice of giving her free rein as a child, and as a result she grew up lacking the self-discipline to curb her whims. She would never be content. She always had men and she was never monogamous. She conducted these affairs flagrantly, in a way intended to shock, and was bloody in her treatment both of her admirers and her parents. I never found her attractive and never understood why so many permitted her to walk all over their feelings. She seemed to derive a perverse pleasure in promenading her variety of lovers around the house. Especially her writers, dark gloomy men, purveyors of the new kailyard parcelled up in less attractive wrapping. She had a curiosity towards squalor which only the affluent can afford, and liked to satisfy this through reading these gloomy books. It was also an alternative to someone with literary aspirations and no talent to move in literary circles. Aside from school periodicals, Rhys' output consisted of an eleven-paragraph short story in a feminist anthology and petered out there. She she cut her losses and became a writers' moll, doyenne and sole member of the Glasgow cliterati.

But it was Audrey who fascinated me most. A shade taller than her sisters, she, more than they, had inherited her father's characteristics. A quiet intelligence mitigated by her mother's humour, a mind capable of discrimination, a certain reserve in the most curious aspects of her behaviour, she presents an enigma. It is part of her charm. She is enormously alluring. Her legs are long and slender, her waist tapered, her breasts full, her shoulders upright, her neck long. She wears her corn-coloured hair shoulder length and swept back from her wide forehead. The face is large, the eyes light blue, the colour of cornflowers. Her nose slants obliquely and gives the face a curious asymmetry that misses being beautiful and lends character in departing from the prototype. Her glance is cool, impartial, intelligent. I see it now as I recall. It is the impression of sensitivity which remains.

I first met her at the time she enrolled for medical school in Edinburgh. She was a girl then, unsure in herself and in her movements. I kept up intermittent correspondence with her for four years. We met occasionally and I considered her my friend. When she graduated I was presented with the spectacle of a woman, polished in her coordination and assured in her looks. It is Audrey on whom my love for a family found its focus.

16

I DON'T THINK Simon Frew ever fell in love with Elsbeth. In all honesty, she is not the type of woman to elicit passion, and would probably disapprove of it should the feelings manifest themselves. It is a sad state of affairs to grow into someone out of apathy. The match was made not because he was too dispirited to try elsewhere, but more from a sense of trying to please. He tried to please both his mother and Elsbeth: his own preference did not even come into the reckoning. His one certainty in the whole affair was the belief that Elsbeth's austere outlook was founded on probity: he would assume her moral ascendancy till proven otherwise.

There is a main Post Office near the University. Borough residents, whenever they can, conduct all their transactions locally. The sub-Post Office, which Simon's mother ran upon the death of his father, is more convenient. Mrs Frew the elder had no desire to work behind a counter for the rest of her life. During her working period she viewed herself as a custodian till Simon should come of age.

When his schoolfellows flocked in droves to become tradesmen, Simon graduated from school to counter and accepted his patrimony without complaint. It was a dull, dull inheritance which he was constantly reminded he should be grateful for. He did not demur. While his contemporaries hammered hot rivets, planed doors and wired state rooms, he sold stamps, issued application forms for provisional driving licences and weighed parcels. There is no sense of camaraderie to be obtained from selling postal orders. His friends remained constant, for he was liked in his diffident way. Of an evening he would sit drinking with them, listening to their riotous anecdotes of factory life, and smile his quiet smile.

Elsbeth was not slow to realise what she had on her hands. The secretaries with whom she had obtained her diploma were a frivolous bunch. She had had a few social evenings with them where she remained demurely sober. The dance hall had seen them in a group, dwindling one by one as the men extended invitations. Conspicuously alone, she had bought and gagged on a gin. She left, determined that hers would not be a man's world.

An accustomed routine began. Since she left the house at the same time as Simon, Elsbeth accompanied him as far as the bus stop; and since she made up sandwiches for herself every evening, she made his up also. For years he secretly disposed of them to the local dogs rather than forego his lunchtime interlude in the bar. It took a decade of outsides and potted meat paste to work up to an admission. Sometimes she would accompany him to the local cinema. His mother and Elsbeth became thick as thieves, took tea and went to church together. Combined they presented a potent moral force. Without realising the serious nature of the transition, he began to suck polo mints on his way home from an evening's drinking to cover the stale beer he exhaled.

Elsbeth's colleagues in the typing pool accepted proposals of marriage as they had invitations to dance, and again she was left singularly alone. She redoubled her efforts. They visited more cinemas and she even accompanied him to the lounge afterwards, sipping a frugal sherry and noting the tawdry furnishings. His friends saw the match as risible, but nevertheless a match. It became a public assumption that they were a couple. Simon's friends called them Mr and Mrs Elsbeth. A joint Christmas card arrived for them both. Simon didn't even notice. Mrs Frew willingly chaperoned. From Elsbeth's standpoint the whole affair had an incorrigible propriety.

And then Simon's mother died. She had been more demonstrative than the new Mrs Frew was to become, and he felt an irrecoverable loss. But he bore his grief stoically and in private. Elsbeth felt thwarted: she had become fond of the elderly lady whose tastes pleasantly coincided with her own, but news of her death summoned in Elsbeth's mind images of a slumberous Ayrshire village where she would type and crochet, until she too died. The service was conducted with appropriately sombre pomp. A light drizzle began as the coffin was lowered and Elsbeth looked askance at the sky. This added insult to injury. Why? Oh Lord, why? What does it mean to be a good woman? Help me to understand these impediments you have chosen to put in my way.

One of the workmen loitering beside the pile of earth irreverently lit a cigarette. Both were in a hurry to complete their task. The rain was constant through the obsequies, intensifying to a steady downpour. The congregation hurriedly dispersed with muttered condolences to Simon. He turned from the graveside to see Elsbeth gazing at him through the rain. With prudent forethought she had brought with her a man's umbrella, his umbrella, which she put up and gestured him to shelter under. She took his arm. His only suit was sodden. Taking his cue the gravedigger began walking towards the hole with his companion. The first heavy sod hit the coffin while Simon was within earshot, setting up a reverberation in his heart which lasted for months. Assuming he was unobserved, the gravedigger threw in the end of his cigarette with the earth. Elsbeth saw this at the same time as she felt Simon's spasm of grief. Detaching herself and taking the umbrella with her, she accosted the workman and subjected him to a tirade on his profanity that lasted till Simon's vest had realised its full osmotic potential. This was followed by a caustic letter to the funeral directors which secured the man's dismissal and a ten per cent discount. She had already begun to view the family collateral as their finances.

Being handless, he found Elsbeth indispensable in the weeks to follow. She, for her part, readily busied herself with the occupations left vacant by the mother's absence.

When she proffered her rent, in cash each Friday, he absently waved the notes away. The insurance settlement had left him with a modest proficiency after the mortgage had been paid off. Life went on. He was quite prepared to let things continue in the same vein, but the circumstances did not suit Elsbeth. Two single people of different sex and of an age to invite speculation living under the same roof! Did she imagine the sideways glances cast in her direction in the Kirk of a Sunday? So she let Simon know she would begin to seek alternative accommodation and did not elaborate. He was perplexed, wondering what he had done to give offence. Anticipating her departure he thought he had better master the rudiments of cooking. Coming home from work one evening she found him clumsily rolling pastry with a milk bottle. This attempt at self-sufficiency was a horrible presage. Her plans were in splinters and her manly heart caved in: she burst into tears. Simon was horrified. He had never seen a woman cry. He attempted consolation, putting his arms around her and leaving visible handprints at every contact. She said she must leave. He said he wished she'd stay. She said she could not remain under such circumstances. He asked what circumstances? She said people were beginning to talk. He had no idea what she was talking about but said, with more resolution than he felt, that they'd soon see about that. She asked if he didn't think it better that they put an end to the rumours. Still perplexed he said of course. She asked if she could stay. He said he'd be delighted. At this she burst into a renewed fit of tears, wrung his hands, kissed his lips, gladly accepted, disengaged herself and retired to her bedroom to remove the flour from her suit. He returned to his pastry ruminating over the female psyche. Every female caprice that he was unable to understand he put down to menstruation, something secret, ineffable and totally beyond the grasp of masculine understanding.

Next afternoon Mrs Munroe sent a parcel to the Mull of Kintyre and offered her warmest congratulations. He walked home deep in thought. Elsbeth's parents telephoned that evening, catching him on his way out the door to the Piper's Lament. They had of course heard all about him from Elsbeth as an up-and-coming young man. They wished him all the best. He thanked them before putting down the receiver. Elsbeth was nowhere to be seen, probably out somewhere compiling a bottom drawer.

With hands plunged into his pockets and deep in thought he sauntered down the hill. His ambitions, even at the age when young men are customarily most passionate, were modest: proportion in architecture and harmony in human relations. A drink was waiting for him upon his arrival.

"What's new?" said David.

"I'm engaged," replied Simon, with absolutely no intonation whatsoever.

In respect for the late Mrs Frew, Elsbeth thought it only proper to allow a reasonable time to elapse before the wedding took place. During this period decency demanded that she find alternative lodgings, down one flight of stairs and across the landing from Simon. Her visits were frequent, to burke his attempts at self-sufficiency. Her presence was intended as a constant reminder to him of his new status.

As far as Simon was concerned being engaged was something akin to being a vegetarian: a state of existence, more of an end in itself than a means to another end. Elsbeth was happy making plans, and he was happy to leave the arrangements to her. He felt no different than he had prior to their fateful interview. Two nights before the wedding his friends got Simon deplorably drunk and left him ambling the streets at midnight minus his trousers. It was a tame initiation by Borough standards but it horrified Elsbeth. Fearing a repetition she saw to it that the reception was a frugal affair.

Simon's friends left early, repairing to the nearest pub to become riotously drunk, lament the passing of a single man and invent cruel anecdotes of the couple's sexual congress. Simon and Elsbeth adjourned to a hotel in the city centre, prior to the next day's departure to Geneva, a Calvin tour she had arranged as a honeymoon in the steps of her mentor.

So two virgins stood nonplussed when the bellboy departed with his meagre tip. Simon mechanically brushed his teeth while Elsbeth, next door, prepared herself. When he emerged the bedroom was in total darkness, the curtains drawn. He stumbled as he undressed. When he approached the bed she seemed to be wearing more clothes than she had prior to her preparations. Perhaps his friends, two miles away and in jocular mood, were not wrong in their hypotheses over the Frew's morbid consummation.

Whatever happened Elsbeth emerged a new woman. She did not intend to remain a secretary and act out her ambitions vicariously, through Simon. She obtained all financial management. At her insistence the sub-Post Office became a newsagent's also. This meant punishing hours for Simon which she was prepared to tolerate. She also tolerated the sale of tobacco, although a strict embargo was placed on soft pornography. Simon looked wistfully back to his days behind the guichet. The increased workload necessitated employing casual staff. By the time I arrived in the Borough Peter had been taken on full-time. He was diligent enough to earn Elsbeth's approval, but she disliked the idea of two people called Simon and Peter together: it smacked of Popery: her Presbyterianism admitted of no saints.

Despite Simon's open-handedness her plans yielded modest dividends. Finding progressively less and less in common with her workmates, Elsbeth left at the first opportunity. Her small salary had been the pretext for financial independence, which she valued. She kept the excuse alive by taking in alterations as a seamstress. The pin money came in useful. As soon as finances permitted they sold the flat and bought a small terraced house five hundred yards up the hill. Perhaps they could have afforded more, but Elsbeth would have felt incongruous in an avenue populated with professionals. The Borough had never been her spiritual home, and now, on the periphery, in that brief hinterland dividing what she saw as the proletarians from the middle classes, she could look up to the comforting proximity of the University spire and hear its musical peal as it chimed the hours. She never looked down. Simon never looked anywhere else. He lamented the loss of the home in which he had been born, but his work and social activities, namely drink, which he steadfastly refused to relinquish, took him daily down the hill. He moved in the same circles and kept the same friends as previously.

Elsbeth's craving for respectability went unassuaged. But she found herself at an impasse. She found it difficult to socialise with the women up the hill who, in her eyes, had the vicarious status of their husbands' professions. The wives of doctors and solicitors, words always pronounced with reverential sibilance, probably considered a seamstress as equal in their social reckoning to a domestic. There were two fundamentally flawed assumptions which her scheme of things failed to take account of: it was no longer the Edwardian era, and woman could legitimately pursue independent careers. Indeed, the Borough Council, steadfastly Labour since time immemorial, was half composed of women. The teaching profession pullulated with them. Young girls got drunk and fornicated on the way home from dance halls with undisguised gusto. Such things she ignored, finding them inconvenient to her philosophy or corruptions of a predetermined order. The Bible promulgated a patriarchy. That was the natural scheme of things. The glaring contradiction of her own instance also passed by the board. She did not mind ruling Simon, but she minded others being aware of her domination.

She would not look for friends down the hill. Had she not climbed thus far for a moral altitude? She did what she always did, she took refuge in religion.

This faith of Elsbeth's is a fascinating organism. It is a faith shaped more for those it entitles her to exclude than to befriend. It is a peg upon which to hang all her preconceptions and corroborate her prejudices. Although there is a mission towards which she contributes, and on whose behalf she organises fund-raising activities, the concept of foreign worship is something alien to her. Nor will she have any truck with this Pantheist nonsense. Hers is not the God of foaming cataracts, craggy peaks, icebergs, howling gusts or tumultuous seas. She finds something vaguely indecent in any kind of excess. Nor is he the God of Asian multitudes, painted Amazonians or ecstatic African tribesmen. No, he is a white Protestant God who presides over clipped hedgerows and coffee mornings. He is the God of propriety.

What room there was for Simon in that narrow heart soon became occupied by the sombre furniture of Elsbeth's articles of faith. And now, in the Borough, the beast of ecumenicalism was raising its ugly head.

17

DR HENRY CARR produced his new meerschaum with a flourish. We sat in an impressed semi-circle: me, Simon, Peter, Elsbeth, Irene and Carol. Out of the other pocket he produced a new leather pouch of tobacco.

"Henry likes a good shag," Carol said.

Peter spat a mouthful of beer on my carpet. We all stirred in various ways manifesting embarrassment or stifling laughter. I could hear the ice in Irene's glass click as she rocked. Elsbeth stirred her tea pretending not to have heard.

"Virginia?" said Simon.

"What?"

"Virginia?" He now addresseed the question to us all without looking at anyone.

"Who's Virginia?"

The effort had been too much already. He began profusely to blush. It was contagious. I could feel my own cheek warm. An awkward silence settled.

"All contributions welcome," I said, limply.

"My husband's in retail," Elsbeth said. Blank incredulity all round aside from Henry, imported for the night and knowing no better.

"Retail?" He made it sound profound, tamping the tobacco and puffing assiduously. And then again, "Retail?" We all knew he wasn't interested.

"And you?" I asked. I was loathe to give the pompous little turd his opportunity, but anything was better than a semi-circle of social cripples staring inadequately at my revolting carpet.

"An historian."

"Henry reads books," Carol said, "and when he's finished he reads more books. And after that he reads some more."

"And write, my dear," he said, puffing. "And write."

"You write books?" Elsbeth said. It was intended as a question but came out like a spoken article of faith. I had invited her out of deference to Simon, knowing she had only accepted when being told that an academic was also coming. Perhaps she thought he would glide down from the floodlit empyrean in his gown. Had she known of his romantic liaisons she would have dismissed him from the start. Any social venture which included Elsbeth lessened its chances of success. I was gambling on her capacity for snobbish reverence occupying his for flattery. Ideally they could reach their own equilibrium in a corner by themselves.

It was an unostentatious gathering and my preparations were equally modest. A slab of beer, half bottles of gin and vodka for the ladies with a limited selection of soft drinks and my one bone china cup for Elsbeth. Two dishes contained the contents of party size crisp bags. There were some dips and some *crudités*. My clumsy sandwiches made a lopsided pile on another plate. Irene had brought vols-au-vent to heat and Carol a Dundee cake.

Irene scarcely moved or even looked up. She continued to stare into her drink, moving the glass gently from side to side, softly clinking the ice. Each time I scanned the faces I found Simon also staring in her direction.

"What kind of books?" asked Peter.

"Books on how much fun people had ages ago," Carol said. "Books about fun are right up Henry's street."

"I like facts," said Peter. "History's facts."

Henry smiled knowingly and tutted through his teeth.

"Youth . . ." he said, shaking his head in feigned amuse-
ment. And then again, "Youth . . ."

It was difficult not to kick the little shit.

"Professor Carr," Peter began. That wiped the smile off
Henry's face. Carol had groomed us all beforehand with
the story of the chequebook.

"Doctor . . . actually."

Another stultifying silence. Things were not going well.

"Are there evening courses run at the University?" Irene
asked suddenly.

"If you mean domestic science . . ." began Elsbeth.

"Pre-matriculation courses," Irene continued, ignoring
her.

"With a view to studying what?" asked Henry.

"History. Literature. Politics. Who knows? It can't do
harm to know more."

"Of course not." Simon was too quick, too anxious with
his approval.

"Aren't you rather old," asked Elsbeth, "with your children and everything?"

"I'd be a mature student."

No, I thought. With her unsuccessful breasts and ill-
advised shoes Elsbeth would be a mature student. But not
you. Not you.

"I was thinking of when they're older."

"Isn't there a crèche?" asked Carol.

"Who'd trust their children with strangers?" Elsbeth
said, dismissively. Simon seemed imperceptibly to cave in
at this. Was I the only one to notice?

"The option being?" said Carol. Elsbeth flicked her a
glance. Now that she had gleaned their relationship, her
intimacy with Henry had pulled him down in Elsbeth's
estimation. She saw herself as uncompromisingly plain,

and flattered herself on her perception of Carol, with her abundance of cosmetics, as little more than a raddled whore. Elsbeth didn't seem to deem the question worth a reply. For a moment I thought all the glasses seemed simultaneously to shatter.

"I'm sure these people know what they're about," Simon ventured. Elsbeth stirred her half inch of tea.

"But then, what's the alternative? Even if it led to little more than the little I know now . . ." Irene faltered.

"It doesn't hurt to have qualifications," Carol said. "You'd still be young when your children are schooling age." I thought she'd be staring at Elsbeth in retort for the snub, but she too, like Simon, seemed to cave in slightly. There was no malice.

"You're better than eight dozen Puritans!" I blurted, or if I didn't, I should have.

"I hear the waitress in Chez Moira has a degree in sociology," Elsbeth said, to no one in particular. I looked at her. Since Irene had raised the topic of further education, every remark of Elsbeth's had been calculated to thwart this purpose. It wasn't difficult to see why. A woman from down the hill, an ex-shop girl with a violent boor of a husband, a young mother towards whom Elsbeth condescended, trudging daily up and past Elsbeth to the University somehow distorted the social order.

"Around any University there's any number of students doing jobs like that to try and help make ends meet," I said.

"I hear she's graduated," said Elsbeth implacably. "Why bother?"

"There's no shame in being a waitress," I said.

"I've worked that way before," Irene said, "and I'd do it again to subsidise my way through. Provided I was accepted, of course."

At this point Henry gave a preparatory cough. Having listened to all the speculation, he now, having appointed himself as arbiter, prepared to put us right.

"The question is . . ." he began. Carol stood abruptly and turned to me.

"Where's your toilet?"

Peter laughed. She must have been in dozens of such tenement flats. They are built on an identical floor plan. She could not fail to know.

"I'll show you," I said.

We walked ten feet to the hall. I closed the door behind us. "There," I said pointing. If it hadn't been my flat I would have left. I stood, not wanting to return, summoned myself and opened the door. Henry had evidently made some kind of joke and Simon was politely saying "Ha ha ha . . ." in a poor imitation of laughter. My first impulse was to retreat. I stood for a moment.

"Who'd like something to eat?" I asked. Carol was at my shoulder.

"I'll help," she said.

"So will I," said everyone else except Elsbeth and Henry.

We all moved to my tiny kitchen and they all watched me make several attempts to ignite the pilot light. Then we all watched the kettle boil. Irene heated the pot and Carol handed her the tea bags. I distributed hot sausage rolls and vols-au-vent and we all filed back *en masse*. The sandwiches, crisps and cake were all eaten, more for the sake of occupying our mouths and hands than from relish. Elsbeth picked, leaving on the side of her plate some fragments which, for reasons known only to herself, she considered inedible. The couch was soft and we ate leaning forward at an awkward angle. Peter surrounded himself with a carpet of crumbs. When we were almost finished Irene caught my eye, stood, demurely dusted herself off and moved towards the hall. I followed.

"There," I said, pointing. I had even bought liquid soap for the occasion. She smiled.

"I know. This flat's like mine. Like ours."

"Of course."

"I'm going."

"Already?"

"I have to."

"All right. If you didn't go would he come here?"

"If I'm late he might."

"And the children?"

"He'd bring them too."

"And if they were asleep?"

"He'd bring them too."

"All right," I said, "you'd better go. He won't . . ." I floundered, "he won't hurt you."

She coloured. We both thought I'd gone too far. I expected to see her to the door without receiving an answer when she turned and said: "He won't hit me. He never hits me." I didn't look at her.

"Goodnight," I said.

When the door closed I had no further reason for not going back. They must have heard the sound of the shutting door in the lounge. When I returned Simon looked up at me expectantly. Strangely enough, I'd interrupted a conversation. Elsbeth was being adamant.

"It's unnatural!"

"That begs several questions," Henry replied. I glanced from one to the other.

"Homosexuals," Peter explained, cheerfully. "Some of Henry's colleagues are homosexuals. We were wondering if there are as many down here as there are up there and it's just that people keep quiet about it."

"Attitudes are a question of vogue," Henry said. Now it was Elsbeth who coloured.

"I won't pretend to know what you're talking about, but I know it's a filthy degrading act carried out by filthy degrading people!"

Simon moved towards me. I grasped him by the elbow and dragged him into the hall.

"There." I pointed at the toilet door, almost shouting.

"Why did she go?"

"She's apprehensive about leaving the children too long."

"He won't . . ."

"No. Go to the toilet. Even if you don't want to. Go in and flush the cistern."

Behind me two voices were raised. I watched the door close behind Simon. I stood still and felt a momentary desolation: Simon in the toilet, Carol abstracted and Peter cheerfully watching an argument while a zealot shouts down a snob. And this was representative. A trivial soirée that didn't work and didn't matter. And yet I was wrung.

Was it for this I came?

18

THE PATON FAMILY live in the village of Kirklee, ten miles west of Glasgow. Two minor highways, coming from the direction of the coast, converge into a single metalled road, paralleling the train track which leads to Glasgow. In the commuting hours there is incessant traffic. During the day the village is given over to children and the elderly, anyone else abroad during working hours appearing truant and incongruous. At seven and after weekends the traffic is intermittent.

The village is bisected by a main road. On one side lies the council estate, erected with utilitarian disregard for privacy and what light industry remains. On the other, aside from the coach house, a preserved weaver's cottage and remnants of the older settlement, lie the older houses, built at the turn of the century, spaced at humane distances from one another. An aerial view of the village reveals the discrepancy.

The village grew up around the weaving industry, producing muslins, ginghams, cambrics and lawns. Nowadays, besides the paper mill and paintworks, little work is provided locally. Some of the locals find work in Johnson or Paisley, or in the industrial towns on the edge of the Glasgow conurbation. Of the affluent, almost all, without exception, travel to Glasgow, some to Edinburgh, fulfilling their professional status and earning enough money to allow them to live in the village. House prices in desirable outlying districts have reached an exorbitant premium. Speculators bought and converted some of the older villas into executive flats. At the time of my acquaintance with Kirklee a new social stratum had emerged, that of the young executive who left early, returned late, drove fast cars and housed fibre-glass boats in convenient placid lochs. I am not close to local opinion in the village, but I understand the change has caused resentment. It is an ancient place going back to sixth-century colonisation by Irish monks. Old wealth is tolerated. The *nouveau riche* are seen as social pariahs who have not so much evolved as materialised. With their attaché cases and Anglophile manners they have set up a discordant note.

At a junction in the road, a recently constructed estate exists, built by private contractors for families of modest means. Such estates proliferate in England, consisting of similar houses which the owners immediately try to individuate by painting the front door a different colour, planting small conifers outside and ascribing absurd names like "The Larches" to. From such modest means the Paton girls sprang. The parents, to their credit, were too discriminating to become involved in this *petit bourgeois* one-upmanship. The father said nothing, assiduously slaved, and with a sufficient sum moved his brood into the house which they now occupy. The transition was easily made. Their idea of social deprivation is a shared bedroom which they have faint memories of.

Natives of Kirklee, in memory of some eponymous piper celebrated by local poets for his skill, are called Corries. Charis was a Corrie. She was the favourite daughter of a local and wealthy landowner who took a patriarchal interest in the running of village affairs. He celebrated her eighteenth birthday with a fête and local pageant and mobilised the village enthusiastically to participate. They have been doing so every anniversary since. Father and daughter have long since died, but little Charis has ousted the piper in civic memory. She bequeathed us Charis day.

The Paton girls cannot remember a year without Charis day. It is part of their internal calendar, and another family foible which cannot be shared with outsiders. Audrey did her best to incorporate me. She has also shown me the family scrap book filled with pictures of successive Charis days. The first shows the girls as infants, dressed as blackbirds, sitting upon a float in the shape of a huge pie from whose crust they emerge, wheeling down the main street. Each year they are a little older and the costumes more elaborate. They relate stories of their mother, with infinite patience labouring over a sewing machine the night before, running up outfits to her daughters' specifications. It appears to have been a labour of love. Sometimes she is there with her girls, lambent-eyed, her hand on their shoulders. At such times she assumes a beauty entirely her own. The father never figures. At fourteen Rhys disappears from the photographs. Audrey stops at approximately the same age. Katrine endures a few more years and, unwilling to go it alone, joins her sisters. Although not part of the pageant they have attended ever since.

When I arrived at the train station it was early on a Saturday spring afternoon. The sky was brilliant. Dragged from my tenement existence I looked around with some dismay at the bursting world. In the rolling green of the fields was a vivid yellow parallelogram of rape. For a country destination the train had been unexpectedly busy. When they all disembarked with me I realised that they too had come to celebrate Charis. The train station is small, a single perspex lean-to in either direction. No ticket office. I let the crowd disperse, surveyed the fields and clutched close the chocolates I had bought her mother. At my age I had no excuse for nerves.

I followed the stream of pedestrians, mostly mothers and children, towards the open field where I could see the marquees and stalls erected. Audrey had told me over the telephone that we would never find one another in the throng. I was to use the fête as a landmark. Candlehill Road led off at an obvious tangent, upwards and to the right. Theirs was the last house but one, on the crest of the hill. She would be there, perhaps with the family.

There was a trickle of people coming in the opposite direction, again mostly women and children, carrying with them booty from the fête: miscellaneous pieces of domestic rubbish from the flea market, dog-eared paperbacks from the book stall, cheap plastic toys from the bran dip and more of the like. One family in particular attracted my attention. A large woman, perhaps in her mid-thirties, pushed an infant in a pram, while behind her ambled her son. She was a heavy woman with a florid face, perspiring at the exertion of hauling her own weight towards the station. She wore a short-sleeved T shirt on which was a logo advertising Charis day. Two thoughts immediately struck me: had Charis' father realised he would start another cottage industry, and how did she manage to find something to fit? The infant in the pram was dressed in white, giving no clue as to the sex. The boy bringing up the rear was about four years old, and dressed in a costume of the Arabian Knights. His mother had clearly gone to some trouble, but her patience looked near its end. He ambled, as children do, like a dog finding distractions to left and right. In his right hand he held a five-foot string, attached to the end of which was a helium-filled balloon, bobbing to his springy gait. I nodded to the mother as I passed, who smiled and gasped out an affable reply. The boy looked at me with open-eyed childish curiosity. I passed on.

A loud wail stopped me and I turned round. The child's cry grew more shrill as the balloon ascended. The mother interrupted as it breasted tree top level. I heard her promise him another and offer several more incentives until her patience broke. I heard her take him by the hand and march him towards the station. I heard the sound recede and all the time kept my eyes fixed firmly on the balloon.

There was no wind and not a scrap of cloud. It ascended

vertically, the cord hanging perpendicular. The lane leading to the fête was overhung by a canopy of branches. It negotiated the obstacle of their stretching boughs and rose steadily. Keeping my gaze on the balloon I walked to a patch not obscured by shade. The sky was translucent blue and the light poured down. Up it rose, a dot against the blue vaulting, then a pin prick, until it disappeared completely in the impartial expanse. I drew my eyes away towards the yellow rape and the green trees and the box in my hands and felt a wave of self-reproach. Was it for this I came? The blare of a Tannoy announcement broke in upon my thoughts and I turned towards the metallic sound. Unbidden, a steward approached and thrust a paper into my hand. I smiled my gratitude. He remained immobile until I realised he expected a subscription of some kind. I pulled what loose change I had from my pockets and handed it across. He thanked me and moved off. Some time ago, looking through some old photographs, I rediscovered the paper lying crumpled at the bottom of a shoe box. I flattened it and reread.

CHARIS DAY PAGEANT

SOUVENIR PROGRAMME

STALLS GALORE
Tombola, Wheel of Fortune, Honey & Home Baking, Nearly New, something for everyone.

MISS MOPPINS GYMKHANA SPECTACULAR
Watch the young Kirklee equestrians put through their paces.

BABY SHOW
Prizes for biggest and most beautiful.

DOG SHOW

Prizes for best appearance and best behaved.

CARDONALD BATON TWIRLERS

THE KIRKLEE CORRIE FLEMING PIPING CHALLENGE

OCHENLEICH SYNCHRONISED KITE DISPLAY

GRYFFE VALLEY BRASS BAND

CROWNING OF THE CHARIS QUEEN

And much, much more!

I found the entrance to the fête and took my bearings. Inside, between the marquees, I could make out some civic official wearing his chain of office. Having had no previous experience of the affair, I thought the whole thing looked like a roaring success. A general atmosphere of busy hilarity pervaded. I recognised someone from the occasion of the house party, a woman, a neighbour perhaps, diminutive and smiling in the distance. Audrey would be waiting for me at the house. Was her family here? I desperately wanted ten minutes alone with her to orientate myself before enacting pleasantries.

I found Candlehill Road and began walking. The view from the top, over the fields I had just left behind, was marvellous. The rhythm of another train wafted up and I could see it making its slow progress towards the city, bearing, no doubt, the balloonless child. I turned into their driveway.

The house was blonde sandstone, two storeys and a large attic high. Large windows on the south side flashed back the afternoon sun. Entrance was by an arch recessed in the gable end. The drive described a circle completely round the house and garage. From where I stood I could see strawberry netting covering the freshly turned bed. There was a small greenhouse and a carefully wrought pergola which struggled against the rigours of the Scottish winter. A garden seat against the south wall had been placed to make the most of the light. In summer they read here. There was a small copse of trees overhanging a slight depression with sparse shrubbery. Katrine tells me this is where they have buried the generations of pets the girls out-lived. Gerbils, hamsters, rabbits and whatever small mammals they were permitted as pets silently putrefy here, interred in collapsed shoe boxes, buried among small girls' tears with as much pomp and consolation as parents with no eschatology can muster. I took inventory at a glance and began walking with heavy feet, crunching over the small stones of the driveway. For a reason I couldn't fathom, I wanted her mother's approbation. I wanted it even more when I saw the pictures of her lavishing love on her three girls. For the father's opinion I neither knew nor cared. I approached the door desperately clutching my chocolates. The bell sounded far away, as if from the distance of some stony vault. In the silence which followed I could hear the hammering of my heart.

I heard no footfalls. Audrey answered and smiled me in. I stood at a loss in the hall and felt obliged to say something.

"The family?"

"At the fête."

Thank God.

"Chocolates," I flourished them, "chocolates for your mother!" I was shouting.

"Perhaps you'd like to give them to her yourself?"

"Yes."

"Would you like to take off your coat?"

I made a mess of this, trying to slip the sleeve over my

wrist while my hand steadfastly refused to relinquish the box. She placed the chocolates on the hall table and took my jacket, hanging it in an alcove. She came back and seemed to study me for a moment.

"If you were my guest, and I were you, I'd kiss me," I said, with a bravado I didn't feel.

She smiled, slid one hand under my arm and across my back. With the other she cupped the back of my head. I think my arms hung lifeless. She kissed me and I closed my eyes. Then she kissed me again. I wondered for the first time if I was attractive.

"Would you like me to show you the house?"

"Yes, please."

She took my hand and led me from room to room. I remember books and more books. A plethora of books. She showed me the upstairs first. The staircase was wide and two-tiered, framed on one side by an oak balustrade. Mullioned windows stretched to the upper floor, leaded panes of blues and greens and ochres casting a coloured twilight on the half-landing. Like the stairs all the floors were polished hardwood, scattered with occasional rugs.

On the upper storey she showed me her parents' bedroom first, avoiding her sisters' for reasons of curious discretion I did not understand. It contained an enormous bed and large pieces of incongruous furniture dwarfed by the room they were intended to occupy. The bay window faced west. The vaulted ceiling had been gaudily painted in a manner I did not care for. Still taking my hand she led me into her own bedroom.

There was no question of attempted seduction. That was not why she had brought me. It would have been impossible, her bed, the same she had had since a young girl, scarcely wider than her narrow shoulders. The whole room was a shrine to her childhood. She was incapable of throwing anything away. Artefacts from her teens vied for cupboard space with the hanging dresses and the toys of infancy. The whole place was a curious mélange. We sat on the floor and she produced innumerable scrapbooks. It was here I saw the photographs of past Charis days, and read the halting entries, marred by reticence, that each of the girls had contributed to their school magazine. There was adolescent poetry too, demotic, ingenuous, touching. I felt abashed at having no such mementos to exchange for the touching courtesy of these privileged glimpses. She took me by the hand and led me downstairs.

The father's study: books, an enormous leather-skivered desk, antique typewriter and a collection of equally old Leica cameras. The lounge: books, leather suite, coal fire with brass accoutrements and the same expanse of glass as the parents' bedroom directly above. The kitchen: hygienic, panelled in Norwegian pine with dropped ceiling of the same material, stripped pine furniture and a superfluous row of bells with which to summon servants. Outhouses with a second freezer; drying room given over to Katrine's artistic bent and decorated in murals of her own design. Finally the maid's room, now redundant, given over to housing the miscellany that could not conveniently be housed elsewhere. There was a sewing machine in the corner surrounded by patches of calico and other materials I could not identify. Draped across a chair was a strapless dress of some layered diaphanous material.

"What's this?"

"It's a summer dress. I made it."

She had her back to the window, both hands resting lightly on the sill, one foot protruding slightly further forward, knee slightly crooked. What light percolated through caught her hair in a soft corona. I felt seized by a sensation I had never previously experienced. The gap and the silence between us seemed charged. There was something inevitably right. With no self-consciousness whatsoever and making no attempt to leave I said: "Please try it on".

She looked at me thoughtfully for a minute and then smiled. Pushing herself off the window ledge she crossed her arms in front of her, took hold of the waistband of her top and began to inch it upwards. At the sound of the front door she stopped. Perhaps my expression spoke volumes. She took my hand and gave me a rueful smile. I summoned myself.

"The chocolates," I reminded her.

19

I AM WORRIED about Peter. An observable prognosis has emerged in his drinking. Come five o'clock on a Friday, as Simon shuts up shop, Peter precedes him to the bar and sets up two drinks. Simon arrives and Peter practically inhales the first pint at the relief of being released from the tedium. Not that these two do not get on. On the contrary, they have a great mutual fondness. Peter buys the first drink, quaffs it to the dregs and Simon, barely two sips beyond the foam, reciprocates. Peter downs his second with no slackening of relish. People arrive: sometimes Tom, sometimes David and others. Peter is foolish with money. He cannot see beyond the evening ahead and he has been paid in cash. I have taken him aside before.

"It's only eight o'clock."

"Wha – a."

"How long have you been here?"

"Five."

"Since five?"

"Since five," and a sagacious nod.

"How much money have you left?" He shows me. It is pitiful. He has no one but himself to account to and will suffer the consequences of his spendthrift ways without complaint. When he has money he is generous to a fault. When he is poor he is nowhere to be found, lingering in his bed-sit without bitterness at his largeness of heart going unreciprocated.

"Go home."

"Home. What's 'home'?"

"Have you had anything to eat?"

"Not hungry."

"Come back to mine and I'll make us something. If you want we can come back here afterwards."

"The night is young!"

"And so are you" I have to restrain myself from saying.

By seven o'clock on a Friday he is cheerfully drunk. He speaks loudly, loves everyone and gesticulates in an exaggerated fashion. By eight he is generally maudlin. Half past nine sees him hitting his second wind, with a joyousness on the verge of desperation and a febrile brilliance in his eye I cannot bear to look at. Half past ten finds him in a melancholic stupor that lasts till he is evicted at closing.

In the past his drinks with us were a preamble for the night's proceedings with friends of his own age, friends who danced and drank and flirted and screwed and did all the things proscribed them in their early teens. I have seen them, in the Borough dance halls and streets and bars, blazing like comets in a fated adolescence, more passionate for being brief and more frenzied still in the knowledge of its own transience. This is as it should be.

Of late, as they grew older and partnered off, he has abandoned his outings and sat rapt in false *bonhomie*, automatically sipping. I have told him there is nothing for him here.

"Go with your friends."

"These are my friends."

And in this bibulous camaraderie he squanders the most poignant moments of his life.

He drinks as if anticipating prohibition. It is one thing to drink for the novelty of intoxication at seventeen: another at twenty-five. And he has managed, in his first quarter-century, to fall into a routine it normally requires the better part of a lifetime of disillusionment to establish. He is lonely and getting lonelier. I can feel it. And he thinks his chances of happiness are receding at every aborted romance. He is lost. In this we are kindred spirits. His drinking is symptomatic.

I am worried about Peter.

20

"THE EC-U-MEN-I-CAL movement!" A vociferous staccato of monosyllables. "The ec-u-men-i-cal movement!" A Glaswegian Lady Bracknell. Had she known, the comparison might have pleased Elsbeth. "Where? Where was this heard?"

"In the bar," said Mrs Simms. She and her two

companions had been taken aback by the reaction they had elicited. On hearing the rumour they had immediately scurried to Mrs Frew, expecting her to be as pleasantly scandalised as themselves. A small coterie of women in the congregation enjoyed nothing as much as a good illegitimate pregnancy or marital rupture to warm their hearth. But this . . .

"The bar!" Elsbeth turned on Mrs Simms. "The bar!" as if the harbinger of news was guilty of loitering there herself. Everyone knew Mr Simms spent less time at the bar than Mr Frew. "I might have expected it. Filth emanates from filth. And who do they propose to admit?"

"To the bar?" It was one of the Misses Kay who spoke.

"To the movement."

"The Baptists I imagine," said Mrs Simms. Elsbeth's lips compressed no further at this.

"The Muslims do you suppose?" asked the other of the Misses Kay. She had heard rumours of a Shinto shrine in Anniesland. In her confused nomenclature, everything not immediately identifiable as Christian was Muslim.

"Ecumenicalism is a Christian movement," corrected her sister.

"It's a rag bag," said Elsbeth. "Why not the Nestorians? Or the Rastafarians with their ganja? Or the Armenians with their . . ." Her resources failed her. She had tried to learn something to the detriment of every sect but her own to support her Presbyterian hegemony. They waited patiently while she groped. "And I suppose they intend to let in the Catholics as well. Why stop there? Why not Beelzebub himself!"

They were cowed by her righteousness.

"Who was talking about it?" she asked.

"Mr McCullen," answered one of the Misses Kay.

Elsbeth's eyes narrowed. She knew nothing of the family but the name had a papish ring to it. Elsbeth was an expert on religious genealogies. With such a falling off in Sunday congregations, she had recourse to such methods as asking passing children, whose parents she knew, what school they attended, to garner her information.

"He's not a Catholic is he?" asked Mrs Simms.

"He's not a Protestant," said Elsbeth. Her religious xenophobia divided the world into Protestants, non-Protestants and Catholics.

"I don't think he pays any heed," said one of the Misses Kay.

"He's a heathen," said her sister.

"No," said Elsbeth, "he's not a heathen." Her mind was more adroit at framing ideas than her mouth words. Heathens danced naked in jungles with shrivelled animals adorning their bodies, or threw themselves off hundred-foot poles to which they were tethered by jungle creepers. They didn't subvert innocent Protestants in Glasgow pubs. That required rational malevolence: belief and not the lack of it.

"Why would such a boor as Mr McCullen interest himself in anything religious?" asked Mrs Simms. "He never has before."

"He's not a heathen," Elsbeth repeated.

I know McCullen. Elsbeth is wrong. He is heathen. He cares for nothing that will not yield him immediate gratification.

"He raised his voice and thumped the bar – so I hear," said one of the Misses Kay. There is undoubtedly some truth in this rumour. But then, McCullen is the type of belligerent who raises his voice and thumps the bar on any pretext. He enjoys losing his temper.

"Proselytiser," said Elsbeth.

"It's said he quoted a book," said Mrs Simms.

"Dear God!"

Reading aloud was still within the realms of possibility – just.

"And handed out leaflets," from a Miss Kay.

This last remark was a lie. The woman who uttered it knew this to be the case, and so did her two companions who had accompanied her to Elsbeth's house. But it was what they wanted to hear and they colluded to the point of cowardice where, within five minutes, the taciturn bargain of the shared lie was no longer necessary.

"Promulgator," from Elsbeth. Her delivery is at its best in denunciation.

"And spoke to a priest on the way out."

"On the way home."

"Yes, sorry. On the way home."

"And said grace before his pint."

I had been there to witness the incident. The local Church of Scotland minister, a charitable man and free with his time, had carefully established a rapport with the local parish priest. The links had gone as far as interdenominational football tournaments and joint outings to Loch Lomond with fourteen-year-olds, the commendable premise being that, got young enough, there is no need for them to learn bigotry. It did not require much to nullify all the effort. All it took was one incident – like McCullen, leaning across the bar as he bawled an order and spotting the red hand of Ulster motif tattooed on a customer's arm and beginning to shout about Papal infallibility – to polarise the clientele. And that's exactly why he did it. To know him vaguely was to know him capable of any arrogance.

The lies piled on.

"And called the Moderator something I couldn't repeat."

"Offered lessons in genuflexion."

"Said he preferred communion wafers to ice cream."

Listening in silence, Elsbeth's face set.

21

IN THE PAST, I have seen Audrey's flats. Standards in shared student accommodation usually fall to the level of apathetic lowest common denominator. Hers were no exception.

In preparation for her arrival I cleaned everything first and myself last. The toilet pan was so liberally doused with disinfectant I thought it might spontaneously combust. The meal was half cooked when I emerged from the bath and bleached that. The place looked austere with the clutter gone.

Unlike her sister she has remained a vegetarian. My repertoire is limited. My cook books are in the style of Baden Powell. I thought of reducing "Corned Beef Bonanza" to "Bonanza" but thought better of it. By the time she arrived I had baked a respectable vegetable ragout.

At the sound of the bell I felt a momentary fluttering, as I had outside her house in Kirklee, an instant of self-conscious *déja vu*. I opened the door and in an affected phlegmatic manner motioned her to come in.

"All yours?" unaffectedly gazing round. My hall would accommodate a police box. No more.

"This hallway is all mine, as far as the eye can see."

She smiled. My heart dilated.

I gave her the tour she had given me. This lasted no longer than a minute. When I showed her the bedroom I said nothing. A room with a bed, and mine was nothing more, is self evident. She left her coat upon the duvet and cut me a glance I could not translate. I was anxious that everything not only be all right but be seen to be all right. I was clumsy in my enthusiasm. This never happened before. At my age I had no excuse for the gaucheries of a virgin.

I put on some music. We ate in the kitchen. Besides the front door, all others in the flat had been left ajar. The sound wafted hollowly from the lounge, reverberating through the hall and high windowed rooms. The meal was mediocre, the wine and cheeses fine. She drank more than I imagined she would.

"Would you like coffee?"

"Is it real?"

"Don't be so middle-class."

"Can I have more wine first?"

"You can have anything you want."

"Why do you have so many books?"

"Why do you ask such ludicrous questions?"

"I'm incorrigibly nosy."

"I'm a voracious reader."

"Are you well-read?"

"Not particularly."

"I knew you'd say something like that. I'll bet you are. I'll bet you're one of the best-read people I've met. Besides my father, of course."

"Of course."

"Try not to be so supercilious. You're more of a snob

than I am. I'll bet that's why you read so much, so that in your secret pride you can look at people in bars and tell yourself you're more knowledgeable than they'll ever be."

"That's incredibly shallow."

"Most people are incredibly shallow."

I didn't know if this was true. It was the kind of possibility I hid from behind my barricade of books, and salvaged what embattled happiness I could.

"You have a trade. Perhaps even a vocation. You are a doctor. I . . ." I gestured around. "I'm an eclectic."

"Is that a noun?"

"It is now."

"Don't be so pompous."

"'Is that a noun?'. Don't be so pedantic."

"You're horrible."

"You're here."

She digested this for a moment while she toyed with the cheese.

"And so you collect things?"

"Yes."

"Orts and chips and things. Bits of prose and old philosophies."

"Yes."

"And people?"

"No . . . I've never collected people."

"Don't get so serious."

I did my best not to get serious.

"This stuff goes right through me. Where's the bog?"

"Now who's a snob. Inverse snobbery's the worst. I bet you thought 'where's the toilet' and translated."

"Bastard."

She left the room. It was her cleverness I liked most. But this glibness wasn't real. Like her father she had found something to hide behind to establish her equipoise, except that this cordon was socially acceptable. Like Peter, she had the ability to be hurt. When she returned I asked something which had perplexed me for years.

"Why do all girls carry their handbags to the toilet?"

"I'm not all girls."

"More wine?"

"Please." We listened to the pleasant sound as it slapped from the neck into the glass. Then she said, "Why do you have right-angled mirrors in your bathroom?"

"To give the illusion of space and light. That's why they're opposite the window. It's a trick to delude ourselves that there are no confines. Like everything else. Why?"

"It shows my profile." She lifted her hand to her face, as if attempting to conceal or transform its outline. It was not a gesture of vanity but a moment of self-consciousness, a flaw, and that aspect of her vulnerability she foolishly thought prudent to conceal showed through. At her sudden exposure I felt a cataclysm of love.

"Isn't it horrible?"

"No."

Was it for this I came?

21

WHEN THE EVENINGS are long I hear children play in the back courts. They play till the light has faded and shout to their parents: for titbits to be thrown down, for permission to stay out a while longer, for a reprieve from bath night. I see the boys, perched on parapets of bin sheds, daring one another into preposterous balancing acts. I see the girls, unimpressed by foolhardy gymnastics, impersonate the adult roles they will try to escape from twenty years hence. I hear warnings bawled from tenement windows. I hear the inevitable fall, the clatter of bins, the wail, corroborating the shouted prediction: "It'll all end in tears."

The memory blurs; the faces interchange; the children grow no older. The expression has remained with me.

22

ELEVEN YEARS AGO a small girl entered the Borough sub-Post Office. Simon was through the back furtively scraping potted meat from the sandwiches he had deliberately forgotten and which his wife had just delivered. Elsbeth stood alone in the front of the shop when the child entered. A shout through to the back produced no response: he had left the tap running to camouflage his activities. School lunch was almost over. Walking behind the counter Elsbeth took the matter in hand.

"Well?"

"How much to send this to Nairobi?"

"Who lives there?"

"My mum's sister."

"You mean your aunt."

"I suppose so."

"And you are?"

"Bernadette."

There was no need for the surname. Giving a cursory glance at the chart behind her Elsbeth quoted a price. The girl produced the paper the coins were wrapped in, and unfolding began laboriously to count.

"I haven't enough."

"These things cost," Elsbeth said.

"You have enough, Bernadette," Simon said. He was standing with his back to the kitchen entrance, watching the proceedings. Behind him the tap continued to run. "My wife quoted the Asian rate. It's an easy mistake to make."

"How much then?"

"Put the parcel on the scales."

They watched the needle settle. He took the bundle of coins from her.

"Have I enough?"

"Yes."

They could hear the distant clamour of the school bell. She turned to go.

"Thanks Simon." When she had gone Elsbeth turned to her husband.

"Do you even allow children to call you by your first name?"

"Nairobi's Commonwealth rate."

"It's all abroad."

"Not when you're that poor it's not."

"I hope you're not subsidising them."

"Them?"

"Names like that . . . What can you expect." By this time she was talking to herself.

"You didn't even weigh the parcel."

With the door closing on her she shouted over her shoulder: "You've left the tap running."

The incident marked a watershed in their marriage. By that time Elsbeth had become so self-absorbed she scarcely noticed. The significance was not lost on him. One trivial incident. Like Audrey shading her profile it gave him a glimpse of the penetralia, and something broke for him then. The assumption that Elsbeth's austerity was founded on something decent had given him a touchstone. Now he found himself adrift.

He found the world an indifferent place. Ostensibly the same, he continued in his habits. But for the first time in his life he experienced a feeling of self-reproach, not for the bad choices he had made, but for failing to choose. For having allowed his destiny to be determined by whatever fortuitous events shaped it. What he had assumed to be love, without any previous experience with which to compare, he now knew to be merely passive acceptance of accustomed routine. It was a late age to suffer the pangs of romantic disillusionment which normally accompany adolescent angst. With everything in tatters he conducted his life as always, giving no outward sign of this sense of vacuousness. Realising it or not, he began to cast about, looking for something commensurate with his capacity for love.

On the children with whom he daily came in contact, on Peter, on me, on those who deserved it and those who did not, he lavished as much affection as his shyness would permit. I suspect it was from him that Peter learned his indiscriminate hospitality. Simon was too retiring to be reckless. As Elsbeth's more absorbing conversations became increasingly to be with herself, the further out did Simon yearn and reach. And there is one candidate in the Borough with whom it is easy to fall in love.

23

HEADLONG THEMSELVES they threw, down from the verge of Heaven. What I have seen with these eyes.

I have seen the Polar night mass, and watched the dawn skip across the seas. I have watched light fade on Tuscan hills and inhaled the dirty vapours of every foetid metropolis. I have looked down on the sleeping promontories of the Mediterranean, and spread myself across the waving wheat of the American flatlands.

And I have stood beneath the purple nights and breathed my restlessness to the Borough sky. And I have leaned against derelict gable-ends and watched an ancient Cortina negotiate the cobbles. And I have faded anonymously and listened as it juddered to a halt. And I have waited, vexed, bewildered, at the blind human enterprise. And I have listened to it begin, as it always has, as I knew it would. And I have heard protesting springs, as the chassis rocks to the rock of ages. And I have heard the climactic pause and felt grief at dumb generation. And I have watched the misted pane crank down and let the night air in. And I have seen a hand extend, pinching at the neck the fragile bag. And I have watched the viscous blob, refracted in the Borough light, hanging pendulous with its milk, like the pendent world seen from the void when I made my choice. And I have watched the condom fall and belch its contents on the cobbles. And I have heard the rasp of a match, and watched the smoke drift lazily out. And I have seen the ember follow as the engine comes to life. And I have watched the car trundle and seen the tail lights recede. And I have felt pity, lust, frustration. But the point I never understood.

24

A YEAR AFTER Bernadette sent her subsidised parcel to Nairobi, Irene walked into Simon's Post Office.

"Three second-class stamps and a quarter of sherbet bon bons," she said. It was enough. She was eighteen years old. There is no complicated explanation of what happened to Simon. In many ways, with such limited experience, he had the emotional apparatus of a child.

He'd first seen her a few years earlier as a personable girl, and correctly assumed she'd grow up to break some hearts. He rattled out the bon bons, added a scoopful more on a generous impulse and watched her walk out of his shop to ruin herself on a vainglorious lout incapable of appreciating the worth of what he had.

Simon looked for the opportunity of giving her extra sweets again. I was the only one he volunteered this confidence to.

"Keep it to yourself," I advised. "Extra sweets are the kind of thing dirty old men in the tabloids have recourse to."

I don't think the discrepancy in their ages really struck him till I said that. He recoiled as if he'd been stung. It was difficult for him, consciously realising for the first time that he had degenerated to the caricature of a browbeaten husband.

The Borough is small, the bush telegraph effective. It is easy to keep pace with the romantic intrigues of the elect, even when they conduct their affairs with outsiders. About the time I arrived there was a conscious breaking of ranks among the eligible girls of marrying age. Too many had seen their predecessors grow up, work, marry and die within a postal district. New blood was needed to dispel the air of heavy incestuousness which had settled here. Besides, what are the chances of meeting an ideal partner in a catchment area of five dozen streets?

Like all the girls of her age, Irene went uptown on Saturday nights, to the Trocadero, an archetypal tacky dance hall which metamorphosed every few years in a vain attempt to keep pace with trends. Despite refurbishment it always remains tawdry. The clientele remains the same age while the building's exterior crumbles. A Christian Scientist reading room has been incongruously situated next door, and in the narrow alleyway between young men and women take and dispense emergency love to one another in the early hours.

Seventeen years old, heart thudding wildly with euphoria and nerves, tottering on three gins and unaccustomed high heels, Irene made her debut. Alcohol tasted better when illicit; being underage gave the whole situation additional relish. She thought the Trocadero the centre of the world, she thought herself fashionably *outré*; she stood amid a noise like a pulsing miasma, in a crumbling dance hall tucked away in the northern hemisphere, sweating into her acetate dress and thinking what any impressionable adolescent would. And she thought herself unique. As I said, she is easy to love.

She found seventeen-year-old boys even less mature. She had fobbed off three already and was being importuned by another tipsy pubescent when a figure cut a swathe through the crowd. Due to the noise, conversation consisted of a series of lapidary shouts.

Ignoring the fumbling boy at her side, he leant forward and said, "Don't stand here too long."

"What?"

"Would you like to move over there." It was not a question. His self-assurance bordered on arrogance. She cocked an eyebrow towards the boy.

"Because of him?"

"Perhaps. Move anyway."

"Why?"

"Because of the chewing gum in the carpet. All right, don't move. If you don't move soon you won't be able to."

With a curt nod he moved off in the direction he had just indicated, without once having glanced at her temporary partner. Lifting one foot she looked down. Grey strands attenuated from the sole of her shoe to the trampled pile. The same with the other. Disengaging herself as best she could, she followed, threading her way through the bodies and the noise. She felt disorientated by this time. The friends she had arrived with had scattered severally, the great Saturday night romantic diaspora. They had been here before and knew the form. Everyone was the same. There was no solidarity with the possibility of emergency love in the offing. The bodies danced, cleaved to one another, separated, drank, danced, found other bodies. The place pulsed and seemed on the point of combustion. It was a narcotic and she was giddy now. Uninvited, the boy followed in her wake.

The bar was three-deep and presented a uniform wall of male backs. She scanned the ranks looking for him. The boy following, of whom she had been unaware for some time, collided into her. With no pretence of politeness she refused a drink. As he moved towards the bar she moved away.

Despite the throng he had monopolised a table. She wanted him to think their second meeting accidental.

"I was looking for the friends I came with."

"Of course."

"Have you seen them?"

"Perhaps. But then, not knowing them from Adam I wouldn't know, would I?"

"No."

"Just passing through?" This calculated insolence piqued her. She needed some cutting rebuttal which would silence him by its spontaneity.

"Just passing through."

"Take a seat." He offered by pushing one towards her with his foot. After hesitating long enough to wish to seem reluctant, she sat.

"Is your boyfriend lying somewhere stuck to the carpet then?"

"I've never seen him before."

He made no comment and turned to watch the dancers. She felt uneasy. She had no drink. Was there any protocol for this situation? Should she offer him a drink? If he accepted, who should go to the bar? Was it a conscious breach of etiquette on his part not to offer?

"Would you like a drink?" she said.

"What are you having?"

"I don't know. Something different. Would you mind going to the bar? I don't want to bump into him again."

"No need. Waitress service at the tables." He summoned a waitress and ordered two bloody Marys, dispatching the bill with what seemed to her the same aplomb.

"I insist," she said, unsure.

"Do you work?"

"Not yet."

"Keep your money."

He was taciturn throughout and paid for the next drink

also. She felt almost slighted. The music changed tempo, slowing as the lights dimmed further. This was the contrived romantic conclusion, a fifteen-minute preamble before the battery of overhead lights came on and revealed to successful couples the partners they had trawled. Among a devastation of half-empty pint tumblers, lipstick-rimmed wine glasses and replete ash trays, people blinked in the unwelcome glare. Girls with smudged make-up headed for the bathroom and queued to repair the damage. It was a denouement he always avoided. As last orders were called she made a final attempt.

"Let me at least buy you one drink."

"No thanks. We wouldn't have time. Besides, if you have another you'll be sick. You're having trouble sitting up straight. We'll get your coat."

Despite herself she knew he was right. She had difficulty keeping her equilibrium to the cloakroom. When she came out he was waiting. One last look across the throng to locate her friends. He walked on without stopping. Her eyes still had difficulty accommodating to the glare and she could see nothing. She followed him.

The night air stopped her dead. He was standing on the pavement gulping down great draughts. She did not know what to do next. When she joined him he hailed a cab and opened the door for her.

"You should have enough to pay this with all the money you saved on drinks."

"You're not coming?"

"No. But you know where to find me."

Even through the blur of drink the arrogance of the assumption irritated her. She turned round and looked through the rear window of the moving cab. He saw her off with a cavalier wave. If this was a gesture calculated to entice then it was well done. When she was well away she thought up the retorts she was never quick enough to ad lib. At their next meeting, she thought, she planned to be spontaneous, and realised that she had already conceded the point that there would be another meeting, and on his terms. She was half fascinated, half angry at him, more irritated at herself for the ease with which she had allowed him to manipulate the situation. But then, she reflected, she did know where to find him.

For the next two Saturdays he was absent while she systematically reconnoitred, hoping for a coincidence. On the second occasion she allowed one gauche young man to see her home, reproving his tentative caresses in the back of the cab, curtly ordering the taxi to halt three streets short of its destination, before he blundered his way towards an attempted seduction or invited himself in. She was a virgin, and although she did not know fully what to expect, she knew enough to know it was not this.

The next Saturday he found her. At her request they exchanged addresses. It was a balmy night and he walked her home, the green expanse of Kelvingrove a reprieve after the crush and the noise. At the close entrance to her parents' flat he took her shoulder and manipulated her towards him, sliding his hand inside her blouse with a proprietorial grip before he ever kissed her. She felt she should have been outraged, but the ecstatic turmoil she felt with the weight of his hand on her breast was what she knew she lacked with the callow boy in the taxi. Simon, after five insomniac hours beside his rigidly sleeping wife, wandered the streets that night, scarcely realising the existence of the clinging couple his shadow lightly brushed.

McCullen left without making further arrangements. The following week he was almost offensively casual. The

onus of their being together was left entirely to her, and the
pretence of continuous accident was becoming tenuous. In
one respect he was older than the three years which separated them. In her inexperience she found this pose of the
saturnine man alluring. Moreover, when she contrived to
ignore him, she felt nothing but dissatisfaction with the
men she attracted.

The next time he walked her home he asked for a cup of
tea. With some hesitation she led him in, asking him
beforehand not to wake the sleeping family. He threw off
his coat in the lounge and pulled her towards him. Her
sister slept next door, her parents down the hallway. Again
he laid his hands on her before their lips touched.
Unattended the kettle rose to a slow boil in the adjacent
kitchen.

The circumstances were not as she had imagined or
wanted: not propitious. She wanted to reprove him, to
detach herself, but there was in him a brutal voluptuous-
ness which elicited a similar response in her. And being so
close she felt the contained power and rude animal health
emanate from his body. This too was a narcotic.

And so he took her in her parents' lounge, standing first
against the doorjamb, notched by years with the girls'
heights, and later on the hearthrug. It was, for him, merely
another casual discharge. For her the act was fraught with
double significance, desecrating her mother's hearth as she
lay splayed, muffling her response beneath the crucifix and
the watching family photographs as she gave herself to him
completely. The kitchen windows dripped with the thick-
ening steam.

He dressed and left without waiting for tea. She opened
the kitchen window, padded up the hall naked, clothes
bunched beneath one arm, the other hand clasping the

kettle with what boiling water remained. She made the bathroom, found her flannel and washed furtively. There was blood on her legs. The tipsy girl of two hours previously was irretrievable.

25

IT IS SATURDAY. The Catholics are praying for rain. The Borough contingent of the Orange Lodge are preparing their regalia in readiness for the walk. It is the season for parades. Our little coterie of heathens watches from the window of the Piper's Lament.

"All of them at the shipyards," Tom says. "I remember them. Come Friday they ran to the canteen to eat the fish before the Catholics arrived."

Peter is craning at the window.

"For Christ's sake, don't make it so obvious! You any idea how stupid you have to be to be that bigoted? You want them to come over here?"

Sure enough, having dressed for attention they spend much of their time staring belligerently at the curious.

"Where are they going?" I ask in ignorance.

"God knows," from Simon.

"God's got nothing to do with it. If God turned up he wouldn't be allowed in their walk. Too much of a wishy-washy liberal. You have to stoke a hatred like that."

"Speaking of which," says Peter, surprising us with his indiscretion, "is Elsbeth out there?"

"Perhaps in spirit," Simon replies. Since admitting Elsbeth's shortcomings to himself he is loosening up. "But the whole thing's a bit plebeian for her. And it involves drink. They'll march to wherever they're going and then they'll march to some pub."

"They're going to the Convent of the Blessed Sacrament of the Anointed Body of Corpus Christi of the Holy Sepulchre of Fatima . . . Amen," said David.

"You're making that up!"

"Of course I'm making it up."

"It's not so far-fetched," Tom explains. "They're going to march past anywhere with a vaguely Catholic name, hold a barbecue outside Sister Bridget's, burn down her picket fence, get tanked up in the pub and piss on Father Flannegan's garden on the way home."

"All in a day's work."

"Amen."

The drummers are warming, intermittent paradiddles rattling round the square outside. There are some ragged horns also. More people congregate, sweating in their sombre suits beneath the low sky. Sashes, incongruous bowler hats and white gloves abound. The drum rolls are continuous now, a summons. To the novice the whole scene has an alarmingly militaristic air. I can hear flutes too, and at least one accordion. A teenager at the front twirls and throws the long chrome rod up, flashing in brilliant arcs against the sky. A phalanx of some twenty or so masons arrives from the street below, arms swinging in unison, aproned to the knee. Their arrival lends some order and the nebulous mass shudders together.

I can just make out McCullen from the opposite side of the square coming towards us, walking through their ranks unheeding. Even I know this action to be foolhardy. He emerges on the near side having collected only sour glances. It is difficult to intimidate someone of such size. A busload of police arrives to conduct the proceedings, emerging and spreading themselves, a thin blue line on either side of the column. Up ahead, in the direction they intended to march, I can see more police, diverting traffic and ordering aside curious pedestrians encroaching on the route. McCullen continues to bear down on us.

At a prearranged signal the snare drums rap out. Keeping time, the column lift their feet, marching on the spot. A banner of enormous historical inaccuracy is hoisted aloft: a gaudily bedizened man, wearing a tricorn hat and sitting astride an improbable charger, looks down on us while behind him some indescribable mêlée is arrested in mid-skirmish. Their Boyne. This is ours. A flute begins and others take up the refrain. I can see the first drops patter on the window which separates us. McCullen begins to goose step in ridiculous parody. The boy at their head begins to caper, throwing the glittering rod aloft. I watch it revolve in a flashing crescent. He catches it deftly and the column, engaging gear, trundles forward in telepathic unison, like waterfowl simultaneously immersing their heads. The rows of faces wear a similarly bitter expression. The whole spectacle has a kind of repulsive splendour.

Three steps forward the sky opens. The deluge is biblical. Undeterred they continued. McCullen kicks the double doors back on their hinges and stands, glistening on the threshold, demonic, apocalyptical.

"God," he bellows, raising his huge arms to the stained ceiling "is a Catholic!"

26

SIMON WATCHED IRENE live through her trysting days so different from his own. When she had been with McCullen six months she could not imagine life without him. What vague friendships she had had with other men were allowed to lapse. His experience and worldliness excited her. He neither flaunted nor made any attempt to hide it.

"Have you known lots of other women?"

"Lots."

"Have you slept with them all?"

"Most."

"I've never had anyone else but you."

"I know. You don't want anyone else."

"No."

This begged the question of his desires. She was too apprehensive to ask. Having given herself wholly, she fucked with him whenever and wherever she could, fornicating with urgency to preclude him from taking his desires elsewhere. Her zeal and unabashed candour took him pleasantly unawares. He did not appreciate the significance for her of his being the first. Having given herself to him she held nothing in reserve. The first time they spent a weekend alone she came into the room while he was having a bath, soaped and rinsed his back and then, still talking, peeled down her tights, perched herself on the rim of the toilet and voided her bowels. She stopped her conversation only to concentrate while cleaning herself. It did not occur to her to be embarrassed. She wanted to be his friend, his lover, his whore.

He fell into marriage. She had the weight of precedence behind her: generations of women had obtained the sanction she had been brought up to think proper. He fell away from his trade by compulsory redundancy. His apprenticeship incomplete he became semi-skilled, his status proportionately relegated. She worked at that time window-dressing. It was cheaper to live as a couple. His unformed plans collapsed. The refuge he had taken in his undisclosed potential also evaporated. Half her family boycotted the registry office, a travesty of the Catholic ceremony they had imagined for her. He approached the desk with a sense of injured merit. With no one but himself to blame for not living up to his vague expectations, he said "I do" and blamed her.

Within six months she was concealing from herself the fact that she merely rented his fidelity as long as she monopolised his appetites. It was a short-term lease, not an exclusive freehold, and at exorbitant cost to her. The pleasure he had obtained from different women in the erotic preamble was incommensurable. Each had been memorably unique. But in the flashpoint, the orgastic dispersal of the self, he made no distinction. As a conduit for his ecstatic juices one cunt was as good as another. Once he had exhausted the possibilities of her improvised foreplay she was the same as all the rest.

The cooling off was palpable. His lack of concern, of preparatory caresses, of intimation of anything remotely shared, degenerated to his routine of rhythmic emissions when and where it suited. Half torpid, she had been woken by the pain of attempted penetration, and had come to be embarrassed by occasional dryness or inconvenient periods. Her climaxes, with which he never concerned himself, became epidermal. Nor did she look elsewhere, even in her mind's eye. What fantasies she entertained involved him, impossibly vulnerable. She was seeking a wound whose flow she could staunch. Physically he was still the most alluring man she had known. She did not need any other masculine diversions: she needed reciprocity. The only thing he did not begrudge was his seed.

I watched her once, with Simon, as she stood in the half dark, pretending to window-shop while she disparaged her own reflection.

ALL CARPETS MUST GO

So must all self-esteem in the face of unrelieved indifference. I glanced at Simon. His thoughts were obvious: so many people marry the wrong people. "And it's always the same people who get killed in a war," I said, corroborating. She hesitated a moment longer, still without seeing us, then moved off.

"You'd think . . ." said Simon, his voice tailing. Whatever he thought remained undisclosed as he watched her disappear.

"Don't look to the world for equity. You look at her and I know what you're thinking. 'If only'. Don't waste your time with 'If only'. Be thankful there are obstructions."

"Thankful!" This was said with some spirit.

"Perhaps you have a cosy fantasy. And the only thing that lies between you and its realistion is Elsbeth and McCullen."

"That's quite a lot."

"And do you imagine for one moment that Irene feels the same way? Perhaps. But what if she doesn't? What if the obstructions were removed and the thing that kept her away was the fact that she hadn't the slightest romantic notion for you? What then? Looking at it that way McCullen's more tolerable."

"No" he said, slowly. "No. I wouldn't have her unhappy as a sop to my vanity."

"You'd be happy for her to be happy with someone else?"

"I'd accept it. There's no point in us both feeling this way."

There's something humbling about unconditional love. I didn't have it. He was better than I was. Besides, what right had I? Why deprive him of the scant consolation of an improbable dream? Was he made any better by being confronted with the truth of chimerical love?

"I'm sorry," I said.

"You're also correct."

Anyone was worth a dozen McCullens. And he was worth so much more. And she didn't know. There is no equity. I looked around.

ALL CARPETS MUST GO

What cannot withstand must perish.

McCullen's unheralded emissions bore fruit. She interpreted this in the most optimistic light possible, a blood bond beyond dissolution.

"I thought you had protection."

"I have a diaphragm. You know that means my going into the bathroom first. It doesn't make allowance for the times you just come in and wake me up."

He closed the interview by becoming absorbed in rolling a cigarette. She left with the impression that she'd made a baby out of carelessness, by herself, that he was merely incidental.

"A dad by default," he said offering a grim toast no one would accept. "Hers."

Daniel was a difficult birth. She was still going round to her mother's for salt water baths two weeks after she got out of hospital, their own bathroom having only sufficient room for a small shower. The first time the baby woke in the night, McCullen set the pattern by which parenthood in the house was governed.

"Wake up for fuck's sake, Irene! That kid's got leather lungs."

That was all. The nearest he came to affection was a covert pride in the boy's obvious robustness. After two weeks at home each evening, during which he would watch Irene carry the coal scuttle, he considered he had dispatched his duty and returned to his drinking. With the exception of one more person among whom to share his wages, life for him resumed as it had.

His late evenings became the norm. She never knew where he was. The first few times she asked, feeling justifiably offended, she received only vague replies communicating nothing. Given no forewarning she prepared a meal each evening that went to waste two or three times a week. To prove a point she cooked only for herself one night when, by whatever chance, he returned straight from work. She had her reasons prepared; she was ready to discuss the matter rationally, or even give him her plate once the issue had been aired. But she was shocked by the sheer sheet-lightning anger that confronted her when he returned and found one place setting that wasn't his. Her fear of him began at this time. After that she watched, without demur, the food they could ill afford going to waste.

She shouted him down only once: over the matter of Daniel. His bouts of drunken *bonhomie* occasionally spilled over from the pub to home circumstances, his impulsive urges towards her manifesting themselves in sudden frenetic sex or, more rarely, flowers and a variety of carry-out meals. His paternal instincts, dormant when sober, roused him to absurd demonstrations, perhaps to mollify his conscience for obvious neglect. More than once he had awakened the sleeping boy and carried him, half sleeping, through to the front room to relate some drunken anecdote or play an impromptu game. Irene discovered him once, standing in the lounge, throwing and catching Daniel, higher each time, the boy's face rigid with fear. She shouted McCullen into subdued resentment. He left, closing the front door with a bang that shook the building. She realised that such displays of false affection, in someone who enjoyed giving rein to caprice, were the other side of the coin from violence. Daniel became more frightened of his father than she was.

For almost a year he mellowed. Like his erratic night life, from which she was excluded, she discovered no cause for this change. The occasional gifts became more frequent. She assumed that, in his taciturn way, he was trying to make some redress. Even his love-making became less brutish. She began again to relax into him. With the connivance of her mother she resumed part-time work and formed new links. Even if the majority of her evenings consisted in watching the world from her bay window, many were now spent in company. For the first time in years her horizons extended beyond anticipation of the weekend. She began to make plans, none of which anticipated her inopportune fertility.

She thought the news hadn't registered when she told him. He evinced less feeling than on the previous occasion, taking what money remained on the mantelpiece and walking out. She settled Daniel for the night and sat looking out the window, lights in the lounge subdued, wondering how real people conducted their lives and what momentary desolations occurred in the rows of curtained flats across the way.

Strangely, it was the more difficult pregnancy of the two. She worked for as long as possible. He considered illness of any form self-indulgent, and felt distaste at her nausea. When they could no longer make love his time-keeping became as erratic as it previously had been. In her wretchedness she looked at every passing woman as a possible usurper. In the company of her friends she seemed abstracted, wondering who he was with as Elizabeth kicked a tumult in her belly.

She was delivered after thirteen hours of stoical labour. She felt the humiliation of his absence as acutely as anything else. The nurses were discreetly uninquisitive, confining their remarks to deft congratulations. The smudges under her eyes which had disappeared shortly after Daniel's birth remained. Elizabeth left on her mother other indelible traces: the fine striae on her stomach and her almost perpetual weariness. Irene's fatigue had more to do with the emotional indifference she had to contend with at home than the added workload of another child. Work, even part-time, was ruled out of the question by the family doctor, at least for the immediate future.

Despite the shortages, and although he would not admit it to himself, McCullen enjoyed the part of sole benefactor. It had several advantages: it allowed him to remind her of their dependence when it suited, it gave him some kind of touchstone which his restlessness craved, and, most importantly, it provided an excuse for all the unrealised possibilities.

Like half a hundred other botched provincials I could point to, McCullen believed he was painted for a broader canvas. His proportions were heroic and he was dauntless. But if he was incapable of physical fear he wasn't incapable of spite, and that belittled him. And he knew it. Where he wouldn't condescend to dirty his hands on an adversary that wouldn't tax his strength, the rancorous aspect of his nature instinctively sought out the victim least capable of defence. She slept in his bed. He had an arsenal of methods at his disposal, petty domestic antagonisms manufactured to suit, useless on strangers.

So he began to talk about the world as if it was something entirely remote. All the aborted hopes and his prematurely frustrated argosy could be laid at the door of financial commitments, an unemployable wife and two kids. The astonishing thing was that he almost got Irene to believe it. For two years she carried Elizabeth and McCullen's thwarted opportunities till she knew better. The effort all but sapped the natural vitality I saw in her first smile. I met her at the beginning of this dismal interim. She was in the midst of it when we caught her disparaging her reflection.

ALL CARPETS MUST GO

I felt then that had she stumbled forward, I didn't know which of her would have smashed.

27

"SO YOU'RE ON, what's the term, a locum?"

"Sort of."

"You could be a bit more forthcoming. I mean, I'd like to share these things with you, if only by proxy."

"You'd faint if you saw a corpse."

"You don't know the half of it."

She stood up, with her back to the window, one knee

slightly crooked and one foot slightly forward, the way she had stood in the maid's room in Kirklee.

"Are you going to deliver a soliloquy?" I asked.

"You know, you can be a really awkward bastard sometimes."

"And I bought you flowers." I did my best to look hurt. I was nervous, clumsily manoeuvring the conversation to a point where I could work up the courage.

"Where?"

"In a florist. Where else?"

"No, I mean where are they?"

"Cooling in a vase in the kitchen." She stopped. I could see colour suffusing her neck and cheek.

"Really?"

"Whether I did or not, the remark made you pause. You've hesitated long enough to realise there's no call to be angry. There's no need to be embarrassed."

"I'm not embarrassed."

"Well your neck and cheek are."

She strode towards the kitchen but we both knew she wasn't angry by then. I could sense her smile from the back of her head. She returned with the biscuit tin.

"Liar," she said.

"I bought you your favourite biscuits."

"Really?"

"No. But I wish now that I had, which is just the same thing." She sat beside me while we shared the biscuits.

"You don't half talk shite," she said. "Can you imagine if I tried that philosophy with my patients? 'I didn't give you any plasma but I wanted to, so cheer up.' I'd have a stack of disappointed stiffs within a week."

"Are you going to eat all the chocolate ones?"

"I need sugar. I'm in shock at the sight of this defoliated flat."

"So tell me, what is this locum?"

"A house job. You know what that means?"

"Yes. Which hospital?" She told me. It was twenty minutes walk from my flat. "When do you start?"

"Next week. I've finished all the chocolate ones."

"I bought you some chocolate. It's in the fridge." She looked sceptical but the lure was too much. She came back into the lounge unwrapping the bar. She has an insatiable appetite for chocolate which never produces a blemish or an ounce of superfluous flesh.

"There's a kind of rude animal health about you," I said. She nodded in agreement and gave a smile of complicity that didn't stop her jaws. She had chocolate on her lips now and looked like a small girl. "Where are all your belongings now?"

"Here and there."

Three months previously I had helped her move yet again. Just the two of us and a Transit van. She took careful inventory with a sheaf of foolscap and a pen whose end she carefully chewed while I commuted two dozen times up and down stairs to the waiting van below, struggling with boxes of bric-a-brac and the welter of plants. By the time we had loaded up my calves were so exhausted I had trouble controlling the clutch. Then the drive from one Edinburgh suburb to another. Another flat, another two gruesome flights of stairs. Thankfully her new friends helped carry up all the things I'd painstakingly carried down. They offered tea and, when I accepted, presented me with the baffling proposition of four optional blends. Drinking the stuff was almost a ceremony itself. Elsbeth would have approved: fine china, expansive lounge and three of Audrey's new flat-mates, civilised girls taking tea in a civilised suburban room of a civilised city where Boswell had clipped his prostitutes with such relish.

Since then the Edinburgh flat had been used merely as a base as she moved in an itinerant existence from hospital to hospital. Besides Kirklee and her flat, her possessions were spread over half the places where she had friends who could be relied upon to live somewhere more or less permanently. If it hadn't been that I gave her some of my clothes when she was cold staying here, she'd have a repository in the Borough also. When I think of her I see her in my woollen sweater drooping on her shoulders, an androgynous waif till she took it off.

"How is it possible for someone with so little money to collect so much rubbish?" I said, thinking aloud.

"You don't have much. I'd call this place tidy."

"I was thinking of you."

"Oh, really!" If she was irate it didn't stop her chewing.

"Listen, Audrey. I'm serious for a minute. Since you're going to be working near here and shift-work too, do you want to keep some stuff in the flat?"

"What, you mean use this as a base when I'm through in Glasgow?"

"Yes."

"Come when I want and go when I want?"

"Yes. Keep your own hours. I'll give you a set of keys."

"You don't know what'll happen. I collect things in proportion to the amount of space at my disposal. It's got nothing to do with money. I'm like bacteria on an agar plate. Exponential rubbish. I'll absorb the place by instalments."

"I don't mind."

"Your ascetic little flat?"

"Make one of your most glorious messes. Leave your shoes all over the bedroom floor. Litter the bathroom with your lotions and shampoos and God knows what. Hang your rinsed-out tights over the radiators. Leave boxes of tampons in open sight. Eat your funny food and make me some. Fill up the place with your woman's smell. Splatter my flat and fuck me in bed."

And that's exactly what she did.

28

ANOTHER SATURDAY, late afternoon, and McCullen, crapulous, dragging his resisting brood from shop to shop as the shutters are put up in their wake. He is shopping in an aggrieved and half-hearted fashion from the scribbled list in his hand. The sky is low and threatens rain. Irene, uncharacteristically unwell, lies in the dim bedroom nursing a migraine.

A random drop of rain falls on the list before him, causing the lines to blur. He looks towards the bar across the way where the noise of early revellers already filters through to the street beyond. He is considering foisting the children on his mother-in-law. He has only consented to shop under duress. Taking the children is also unprecedented. He wants to drink but his stomach groans in protest. He will need some hot food. He will need meticulously to shop and return home, and perhaps if Irene is still unwell to cook also. He has seldom seen the transition raw ingredients undergo to make a meal, let alone prepared them. He is accustomed to having food provided on demand. All this is an inconvenience. Irene's illness is irritating. Mentally he enumerates all the petty things which conspire to thwart him.

He dismisses the idea of leaving the children with Irene's mother. Assuming she would have them, he knows this would only provoke an irate outburst if he returned home alone. Another raindrop strikes the list, causing more of the ink to run. Half the items remain unbought, and of the remainder he has chosen the most convenient alternatives rather than taken the trouble of going elsewhere for selection. The shops are now closing faster than he can get to them. Irene dispatched him in good time. If necessary they will concoct something or borrow. He is less concerned that the family may go unfed than that he will have no one but himself to blame for their indifferent fare.

Elizabeth is in the push chair. Never having wheeled her before he has never noticed the deterioration of the pavements. His temper is worsening at each kerb and rut. He fumbles the transparent plastic canopy over her as the rain becomes a heavy patter. He looks at the list. Some of the items are indecipherable. Nor can he remember which he has bought.

"Jesus Christ!"

From the window of the bar several can see the frustrated mime. Simon, approaching from the opposite direction, can also see. Looking towards the bar McCullen knows himself to be the object of attention. He thrusts the list into a pocket and jerks the push chair forward. He has not observed Simon's approach.

Daniel's boredom has overcome the apprehension at being in his father's company. When shopping, Irene continually invents diversions to make the excursion interesting. Elizabeth is too young to care. This afternoon the boy has been subdued, following in the wake of the father he scarcely knows. He has allowed the gap between them to widen. Several times already, emerging from a shop, McCullen has had to return inside to retrieve the boy idling at some welcome distraction. And he is not a patient man.

He tries to take stock. He does not know which shops remain open nor what remains to be bought. Encumbered with bags and children any direction he chooses seems immaterial. The sky has clouded; a temporary dark prevails. Crossing the side road the push chair's front wheel collides with the irregular kerb. Elizabeth jerks forward with the unanticipated shock. McCullen swears mutely and looks up at the grey sky, the sodden buildings, the vertical rain and scurrying shoppers in the emptying street. He is over-whelmed by a sense of futility. The smouldering anger which he has nurtured, corroding him day and night for as long as he remembers, wells. A car, travelling the main street at right angles to the small road he has just crossed, puts on its main beam in the gloom. Heavy wipers flick the drops which splatter the windscreen. There is condensation on the inside of the pane. The car seems vacant of human occupa-tion, autonomous, splashing its way through the rain. He watches it, fascinated. The prospect of a dry interior while he stands in the rain with shopping and children intensifies his anger. He still has not observed Simon's approach.

The car does not indicate. The faceless driver shows no intention of deviating from the main street. McCullen turns and is confronted with the spectacle of his son, thirty feet away on the opposite kerb of the side street, stirring the floating litter with a curious foot. The car is about to draw abreast of the man. He sprints towards the boy. The car continues majestically on without turning. McCullen seizes the child by the collar and slews him round.

"You stupid little bastard! You could have been killed! What have I told you about crossing the road!"

The words pour out in a hot welter. The boy is paralysed with fear. He has seen no car, crossed no road and received no instructions concerning safety of any kind from his father. McCullen continues to shout. The buildings are reeling for them both. The boy instinctively raises his hands above his head in an automatic gesture of defence. McCullen is incensed. Galvanised he strikes out. He is slapping open handed, his hands making contact with the child's. The boy screams in fear. The slaps beat time with the syllables.

"How-man-y-times-have-I-told-you! How-man-y-times-have-I-told-you! How-"

"Leave the child alone!"

The buildings settle in their movement. McCullen turns ponderously till Simon, pale and frightened as the child, stands squarely in his field of vision. McCullen loosens his grip on the boy's collar, the unoccupied hand almost gently reaching forward into the gap separating the two men, instinctively finding the range.

"What?"

"Don't hit him again." The words spoken, Simon's mouth twists awkwardly with fear. He feels his body shake. Outwardly there is little movement. McCullen's eyes blur with anger. He can feel pressure pushing outward from the inside of his face. He experiences a moment of complete euphoria, knowing he will permit himself the luxury of an outburst, before his temper unleashes. With instinctive speed and economy of movement the upper half of his torso lurches forward, pivoting from the waist, feet and arms motionless, eyes riveted on target. Delayed reaction of the head overtakes the arc of the body, increasing momentum.

No gesticulation, no signposting, no telepathy. Simon is caught stock-still as McCullen's forehead collides with the bridge of his nose, flattening cartilage and splintering the bone beneath. He folds at the knees, falling like a pile of old clothes, spurts of blood running blackly from both nostrils.

Daniel has run to the push chair. McCullen, at the sight of Simon on the ground, snaps out his trance, collects both children and walks quickly away from the untidiness. Having witnessed the incident the barflys pour into the street. One detaches himself from the crowd to pick up his friend who is kneeling in the rain.

29

ANOTHER PLEASANT afternoon with the immortals in the Kelvingrove Art Gallery. I make my way home at a leisurely pace. The downpour has dispersed the air of heavy oppression. I weather the storm indoors with Sam, the Bengal tiger who died in the Calderpark Zoo in 1964, and is no longer subject to the vagaries of climate.

I come out to a pleasant freshness and the smell of wet earth. It is no weather for introspection. In the distance, weaving its way through the puddles, I can see a strange trio swaying in my direction. Within a moment I can discern a middle man supported on either side by those flanking him.

They had tried to take him back into the bar to repair the damage. I knew the place: a drinking den recently refurbished with glassy ceramics to attract a clientele of office clerks and secretaries. He was sufficiently cognisant to refuse, not wanting his humiliation unnecessarily paraded before mixed company. But his limbs were uncooperative and he was heavier than they had anticipated. They upturned a bin in the main street and sat him there in the rain like some public grotesque in the stocks. Peter produced a grimy handkerchief and proceeded to wipe the blood all over Simon's face. By the time I caught them the third person, a young man of Peter's age, conscripted for the rescue, was staring around blankly making mute appeals to passers-by.

"What happened?"

"Thank Christ you're here," Peter said. "McCullen."

"We'll see to him. Thanks for your help," I said, turning to the young man I didn't know. He had blood on his Saturday evening finery which he was making ineffectual attempts to dab off. With a shy nod to us both he moved away.

"Nice sort," Peter said, as much to himself. I took Simon's face between my hands and tilted it towards the light.

"What a fucking mess," Peter said. "Who would have thought a forehead could do that."

"It looks worse than it is. The face gets a plentiful supply of blood and blood always looks bad." I addressed myself to Simon.

Thickly, "Yes."

"It's six and a half a dozen whether we take you to casualty or to your house. One's as close as another." Simon pushed his head between us. I thought he had some useful contribution to make.

"They're equidistant," he said. I clucked with impatience.

"Move out of the way."

"They say that if the pupils dilate at different rates it means brain damage," Peter said, quite cheerfully. A small crowd had gathered, besides those still staring from inside the bar.

"Listen to me, Simon," he was blinking frequently now, his eyes coming to focus. "We could take you to casualty. As far as I can see you're concussed and I don't think there's much they can do for a broken nose. Admittedly I'm no expert. Alternatively we can take you home and get you cleaned up, and then if you're still feeling bad I'll take you to the hospital. What do you think?"

"Home," still thickly, but decisive. And then: "For God's sake get me off the street."

"Yes. I promise. Take an arm, Peter."

The macabre fascination didn't stop there. Some even followed us part of the way until Peter told them to fuck off. There were also several sincere offers of help.

"Thanks anyway," I said, "but he's only got two arms." By the time we reached the front door his legs had become quite tractable and he was more or less self-propelled.

"How do you feel?" I asked.

"Humiliated."

He had trouble negotiating the few steps to the front door and we again supported him. He handed some keys to Peter who was still fumbling them in the lock when the door opened. Elsbeth took in the scene at a glance. Her composure didn't crack; the severity of her frown became more intense. I later found out why. Five mintues previously one of her cronies had arrived on the same doorstep in a state of climactic anticipation.

"McCullen hit your Simon!"

Instinctively she had brought the woman inside, glancing up and down the street as if suspicious that the exchange had been observed.

"Where?"

"In the face!"

"No. I mean, in public?"

30

I MET THEM IN Chez Moira. When the venue wasn't a pub I knew something extraordinary was afoot. They'd taken a table in the corner and sat hunched severally over the dregs of four cappuccinos, this absurd little cabal: Tom, David, Peter and Ivan. As usual, Tom was talking. David toyed with his cup, lamenting the absence of a pint. Peter looked as he always did, enthusiastic and uncomprehending. Ivan I knew little of besides the fact that he alleged kinship with the Romanoffs, had been turned down by the Foreign Legion and habitually drank a bottle of brown sauce for drunken bets. Tom stopped talking as I approached and dragged across another chair.

"Why all the secrecy?"

He seemed ill-disposed to answer while the waitress hovered near.

"Same again," Peter said.

"Four cappuccinos?" She made no attempt to conceal her exasperation.

"Five," I corrected.

"Perhaps you'd like a chaser?" The sarcasm was aimed at me. Obviously four men huddled over empty cups didn't cover Moira's overheads.

"Just coffee, thanks."

When she'd gone they nodded me to the seat. Ivan was stealing sugar cubes and filling his pockets. The air of spurious secrecy was laughable.

"You four are the first thing anyone in here would look at," I said. "If you'd wanted to attract attention you couldn't have managed better. Why the summons? Why the secrecy?"

"Plans," Peter said.

"Fucking marvellous. Do you think you could elaborate?"

"We're making plans concerning . . ." Tom began, stopping abruptly as the steam machine ceased. There was another tantalising hiatus while the waitress reappeared, clumping down the cups with little ceremony and flouncing back towards the kitchen. ". . . McCullen."

"What about McCullen?"

"Reprisals," David said, matter of factly.

"Reprisals! Against McCullen!" I thought of the man, the corded arms and the hands that could have broken a horseshoe, and I looked at them sitting in front of me, and I took stock. It was difficult not to laugh. "On whose behalf?"

"Whose do you think?" David said. I'd never given Peter credit for the common sense of a dog. Tom was still full of windy bravado at thirty-five, Ivan an unknown quantity. But David, phlegmatic David, should have known better.

"Are you serious?"

"Our best friend is up the hill there nursing a face that'll keep him indoors for the best part of a fortnight. Question is, are you serious?"

"Oh Peter, Peter. Just listen to yourself."

"Ivan says he has a plan."

I turned to Ivan who had graduated to the sachets of

mustard and ketchup now, stuffing them indiscriminately into pockets bursting with sugar.

"Revenging myself on the bourgeoisie," he explained, and then, without further prompting, outlined the subtlety of his scheme: "I vote we call him out and kick his fucking head in."

"That's it?"

"So far."

"Who's 'we'?"

"Well, we thought . . ." Peter faltered.

"Don't! And what'll McCullen be doing while you execute this plan?"

"What can he do?" Ivan asked.

"What can he do? Have you ever seen him angry? What he can do is let his face go slowly black with anger while you all muster your courage to the sticking place. Then he can let his muscles swell with blood till he's half the size again, and go on to kick seven tons of shite out of you, one at a time or all together – it'll make no odds to him. I think he's brutal and he's got a vile temper. I don't think he'd harbour a grudge, but I wouldn't bet my teeth on it. He might go home, have his dinner, remember he is angry and come out and kick fuck out of you all again."

"Put like that . . ." Peter said.

"At the risk of sounding naive, have any of you considered informing the police?"

They all looked at one another blankly. Ivan leaned forward to flick a non-existent speck from the table, a derisory gesture which appeared to be accepted as the general response to my question. It was all too easy.

"Well?" I asked again.

"I hope you haven't," from Ivan. I began to like him less.

"I left it up to Simon. If he wanted to take the matter

further that's his prerogative. I thought so then and I still do. As far as I understand it, there is no shortage of witnesses. I'll help as much as I can. I didn't envisage coming in here and being asked to throw in my lot with Athos, Porthos, Pathos and Bathos."

"No," Tom said, "we haven't informed the police."

"Why not?"

None of them seemed inclined to answer. I left things silent long enough till they felt the drift.

"What is this? The code of the Borough? Do you people shoot from the hip? For God's sake grow up! And anyway, whose benefit is this fiasco for? I dare any of you to say it's for Simon! How do you think he'll feel, up there nursing his face, when he hears person or persons unknown settled a score?"

"It might cheer him up," Peter said.

"Yes. And it might make him think someone else took the initiative because the general opinion was that he couldn't. And the truth is that he stood up to McCullen alone when none of you will."

They began to look sheepish. I stood up. I hadn't touched my coffee.

"You're all doing this to pander to some machismo whim. Simon's just the excuse. Don't include me in your plans and don't tell me anything you do, if you do anything. Are you coming, Peter?"

"I'll see you shortly."

I turned my attention to Tom and David. "He's just a kid, for God's sake."

"Don't . . ." from Peter, considering himself impugned by my appeal. I put down some money on the table for my untasted coffee and left.

31

IRENE STANDS OPPOSITE McCullen, the kitchen table between them, eyes blazing. Rage having petered out with the unprovoked blow, his own expression is one of smouldering chagrin. She refuses to be intimidated.

"He says you hit him. Hit him in public! From what I can make out there was no provocation and you hit him!"

"There was provocation." McCullen says, his normal pitch ominously lowered to a whisper.

"What kind of provocation can a person like that offer?"

"I don't like being told how to conduct myself. Or to unhand my kids."

"What are you talking about?"

"What are you talking about?"

"I'm talking about our son. I'm talking about hitting a child in the street in full view of the Borough. As if being hit wasn't enough!"

"Is that all?"

"What?"

"I fetched the kid a slap for playing in the traffic. Fair enough. He'll have to learn. So what? I thought you were talking about the post boy."

"What . . ."

"Forget it."

"How many people did you hit?"

"Just the one."

"And Daniel?"

"If I'd hit the kid he'd know all about it. Or rather he wouldn't – and that isn't the case. The post boy's probably up there with his smarmy fucking wife. If I'd hit her she'd probably have made more of a go of it."

"Who?"

"What's her name? Elsbeth."

"You hit Elsbeth's husband?"

"Is that what he's called?"

"Dear God!"

"What's the matter? Worried in case you don't get invited to the woman's sewing circle?"

"Why? For Christ's sake why?"

"I said forget it." He begins to roll a cigarette. His hands are trembling, partly from the release of having permitted himself an outburst, mainly in suppressed anger at being catechised by a woman he is accustomed to intimidating.

"You said you didn't like being told to unhand your kids. Did Simon tell you to leave the boy?" Her face is horrified as she realises.

"Oh *Simon! Simon* is it? Maybe you're worried there won't be any more fucking tea parties with *Simon* and that weird bastard who walks around here at all hours listening to everyone, and fuck knows who else."

"I live here! *We* live here!"

"Well we can live here without the fucking macramé set. Maybe you want to go up the hill instead, and swan around the quads, and buy some pictures of water lilies."

"Don't!"

"Well not in my fucking house!" He crosses to the print she has placed beside the pin board in an attempt to alleviate the austerity. "Pre-fucking Raphaelites. 'Isabella and the Pot of Basil'. Not in my *fucking house!*" He rips it from the wall and throws it on the table separating them. She looks at the crumpled sheet.

"Don't. It's belittling. You're looking for an excuse to lose your temper because you know you're wrong."

"I don't need an excuse."

"Then don't. Please don't."

"Not the type of thing Simon would do."

"No." The anger in her voice has been replaced by a vast resignation.

"He is a fucking excuse. Maybe you want him down here."

"Don't. It's weak."

"*Weak!*" In a sudden wrenching movement he throws aside the table which upends and collides with the cooker. A cry sets up from Elizabeth's bedroom. He advances on Irene. She stands resolute, terrified. He stops an arm's length from her then turns, both hands raised to his temples, and stumbles towards the kitchen door, as if spontaneously drunk. She can hear him bumping along the hall, past the front door which he leaves open, down past the close entrance to the outside. She stands for several seconds before righting the table. Elizabeth continues to cry.

32

I LEFT THE CAFÉ in a state of restlessness, gulping the night air, walking aimlessly. The whole exchange had left me depressed. Without intention I found myself standing outside the Kelvingrove Galleries, my path directed there like a lodestone wheeling to magnetic north. The night had settled suddenly, while I had sat with them and their absurd

conspiracy. Inside, frozen in motion, Sam stood gazing piti-
lessly beyond his glass confines into the dim interior; Dali's
Christ hung patiently on his cross; Cadell's behatted lady,
sitting on her chaise-longue with the vivid slash of orange
blinds at her shoulder, regarded the vacant halls from her
canvas; ferns lay crushed into coal; trilobites slept inside
limestone. The immortals, stultified in time. And a quarter
of a mile away four men planned reprisals. And here was I
with a foot on neither threshold. I turned my steps towards
the river.

33

THE PERIOD OF GRIM recuperation before Simon
would venture abroad lasted only two weeks. He found the
time interminable. As if in mourning, or hiding her shame,
Elsbeth kept the ground-floor blinds permanently drawn,
the angled slats allowing only a latticework of light to enter,
even at midday. In this striated twilight Simon felt as if he
were executing his motions in slow motion. The silence
which had fallen between him and his wife had a different
texture to their usual non-committal interludes. They
exchanged necessary pleasantries, and yet he felt something of an unasked question in the tenor of her voice. The
air of those stagnant rooms was weighed with reproach.
The first night, with the occasional wave of nausea, the
gloom of their apartments and his slow groping movements, he went to bed with the impression that he was
living under water.

Peter took care of the business in their absence, as he had

in the past during the Frews' annual pilgrimage to the blustery coastal resorts. Each evening, having deposited the takings in the night safe, he called in on his friend. Elsbeth, making no attempt to dissemble her irritation, showed him into the lounge where Simon was sitting in front of the television. The first evening of his arrival, tea and biscuits, as befitting a guest, were provided by her. By the third evening, once the pattern had been established, this sop to hospitality ceased.

"What's new?" Simon would ask, somehow expecting that world order had fallen into turmoil during his brief sequestration.

"Nothing much," Peter would answer. Planned reprisals were all he needed to conceal. Change, when it came, normally suffused the Borough. There were no outward upheavals.

Their daily exchanges do not bear repetition. The companionship they enjoyed consisted in such lulls and in behaving without affectation in one another's sight. But towards the end of the fortnight Simon began to experience a growing obsession. He thought that the pace of events beyond his front door was increasing, that a conspiracy existed to keep this frenzy from him, and that the more frenetic the world became, so, proportionately, did the pace of his own life slow. Few minds thrive well thrown wholly on their own resources; his was no exception. He expressed his disquiet to Elsbeth.

"That's silly," she said.

His fears were not allayed. He became as restless as McCullen, as restless as me. On his first sleepless night he took to walking vacantly from room to room. He squinted from between the lowered sashes, furtively opened a window and savoured the night air. At the end of the first week, waiting until Elsbeth was in bed, he slipped the latch and walked outside. It was late and quiet. Everything was disconcertingly identical.

"You were out last night," Elsbeth said at the breakfast table.

"What?"

"You heard me correctly."

"Yes."

"I thought we'd agreed."

The embargo on his activities till the swelling subsided and the incident blew over had been more her suggestion than his.

"Yes."

"Well then."

He went out again and walked for hours, meeting no one and returning drugged with fatigue. For the remainder of the night and following day he forced himself to remain awake, accompanying Elsbeth upstairs as she looked in and announced her intention of retiring. It had been years since they had gone to bed at the same time. She looked at him without saying anything then slowly climbed the stairs, he in tandem, two steps behind.

She insisted on his using the bathroom first. He brushed his teeth noisily, purposefully making sufficient noise to announce his toilet complete. He opened the door to find her standing poised outside. She brushed past and snapped the lock closed at his back.

It was her bedroom. The paraphernalia of his adolescence, which she had inherited with her husband, had been secreted by her in instalments to the cupboard beneath the stairs, the box room, the loft, anywhere sufficiently inaccessible to prevent easy retrieval. Whatever youth he had ever enjoyed went with them, rotting in stuffy alcoves. The heirlooms of his father and grandfather, redolent of an earlier masculinity, which had also littered his virgin room, were similarly relegated. Looking round, as if for the first time, he discovered his wife had conducted a process of unconscious emasculation. The clutter had been disposed of: what remained was more grimly austere than any woman's touch he had seen before. His mother's valances, the thick swathe of gathered hangings, embroidered mats for the bureau, the antimacassar and potpourri, all had vanished. The sparse room in front of his eyes defied the accumulation of dust. Everything organic had been disposed of. He sat on the bed, facing the bathroom, infinitely weary.

It was not a place of repose. They had never relaxed into one another. He wanted her otherwise, someone with whom he could lie in shared languor. The discrepancy between his wishes and the reality of the situation was depressing to contemplate. He felt more tired still, remembering their frigid couplings. In all their married years he had never seen her full frontally naked. She came to bed in night clothes and partially undressed under the covers, exposing only what parts were necessary for their consummation. Through a welter of cloth he felt he was penetrating a jumble sale. When he kissed her her lips refused to part. It took him half a year of confidence to slide his hand beneath voluminous folds and encounter an inert breast. On Saturdays their activities ceased before midnight: she said the Sabbath was intended for reflection on the self's unworthiness, not fornication. For years he was rationed without relish. The quota fell when he realised he was being "let".

Tonight, at this place and this time in this dreadful room he needed her. He needed communion, to touch and be touched. She emerged from the bathroom wearing what looked like a cerement, more suited to the sepulchre than the conjugal bed.

She sits on the opposite side of the bed with her back to him, slides her feet from the slippers and hoists her legs under the duvet. Each has a light on their side of the bed. She puts hers out and remains facing away. He leaves his folded pyjamas beneath their pillow and undresses in silence, extinguishing his light as he too slides into bed, his face to her back. He remembers the early years in this position, his attempts at intimacy nestling into her as she craned in excruciating postures from his inopportune erections. It has been an arid match. He moves towards her. She does not stir. He reaches up gently touching her shoulder. She does not flinch. He applies a gentle pressure, pulling her over in a rustle of fabric till she is lying on her back. She regards him implacably in the half-dark. Her face is immobile. He feels vacuous. He would sooner be struck by McCullen.

34

SHE IS KNEELING on all fours, facing the bed head. I regard her from behind, gazing down. The base of her spine is dimpled, two soft indentations. Her buttocks have the full symmetry of a halved apple. I kiss the cleft of her spine and reaching forward cup the weight of her creamy breasts. Her head is hanging forward, towards the pillow, the long nape exposed. I run my hand into the disorderly mass of her hair. I disengage while she remains kneeling, as I have learned to know she would. I slide beneath her, taking the tips of her breasts between my lips.

My clothes lie strewn at the foot of the bed, through the half-open door into the hall, in an untidy trail to the kitchen, one discarded shoe nearest the chair. This marks the path of our urgency. The debris of our meal remains on the table at which we sat, half an hour ago when she gave me the news.

"I'm going on sabbatical."

"To another hospital."

"Yes."

"Edinburgh?"

"New York."

"When?"

"Soon. Next month."

I thought hard for a moment.

"Have you known for some time?"

"I've known for some time I intended to go. The details have just been finalised."

"Forgive me if I seem a bit . . . distant. This is quite a lot all of a sudden. You didn't mention it before."

"No."

There was no response I could make beyond dumb copulation. She understood as soon as I kicked off my shoes. She stood, prepared, sliding out of her clothes as I tore at mine, all composure gone.

Now she is lying beneath me, the crook of her knees in the crook of my elbows as I prise myself from her, gazing down, pulsing with desperation. I sweat profusely. Colour suffuses her face. She breathes in short erratic gasps. She bites her lip. Her feet, suspended in mid-air, flex with the rhythm of my thrusts. Her breasts bob and loll. Her gentle flare from narrow waist to hips follows the contours of a guitar. She is as beautiful inside as out and she has given me access to her beautiful loins. What further admission, I wonder, will be permitted. My imminent climax scalds its way out in a stream of anger and pleasure and uncertainty. She has closed her eyes, the fine lids tinged blue with the tracery of veins. Will she permit this to mean more to herself than a cutaneous spasm? She cradles my buttocks in her hands as I arch for the last time. I look down at the beauty: sweated up, fucked out, hair spilling around in exquisite disarray. Was it for this I came?

35

A KEY SCRAPED in the lock and twisted twice before its owner realises it is redundant. A door pushed open and pushed closed with a breath that flutters the hanging scarf on the rack. A coat shrugged off and left to slump beside its accustomed peg. An interim in the bathroom and a tread across the hall. Irene turns, half-torpid in bed, to see the silhouette of her man loom in the doorway. Through the half-open curtains, passing headlights trace their trajectory across the ceiling. Momentarily apprehended, his face reveals a fixed and baleful look before return to the darkness. Irene, unseeing, turns back towards the wall.

He pulls at his clothes angrily. There is no groping hesitation in his movements to suggest drunkenness. He pulls back the duvet wide enough to expose her also, and clambers in. Roused by the sudden draught she involuntarily shrugs, moving further to her own side to allow him sufficient space. The new patch is cold. She is gradually waking. Her back is still towards him. She sleeps naked.

Like a hibernating animal she gathers more of the duvet around herself, lifting her knees to a foetal curl.

He lies on his back, body rigid, eyes wide, staring at the ceiling. His breathing is heavy, slow, ponderous. The bed moves in concert with the expansion of his lungs. At each suspiration his dense body sinks further into the mattress. Beneath his skin his muscles tense to the point of cramp.

With a spasmodic jerk he turns on his side, facing his wife's back. The movement seems almost reflex, executed without volition. He is two feet from the form of the sleeping woman. He does not approach. His right arm extends, sliding his hand knife-like between her thighs, cupping her pudenda with splayed fingers as he pulls her back towards him. She is startled by the movement and force. The pleasant floating sensation on the verge of sleep she experienced a moment before has vanished. She can feel the swell of his erection against her buttocks.

"It's my time," she murmurs, facing the wall. "You know it is. You know we can't."

He places his free hand between her shoulder blades, palm across her spine. Pulling with the hand between her legs he tilts her body, as if on a fulcrum. Her knees are still raised. For the first time she feels exposed. A surge of fear racks her.

"No!" she begins to lower her legs. His hand between her legs pulls at the protruding string of the tampon. The left hand slides up to her head, twisting a coil of hair around his bunched fist. Gaining purchase he thrusts into her. She screams in fear. The discharge of accumulated blood smears them both. He pulls her hair inexorably till the scream is strangled with the backward pressure on her larynx. He continues to thrust, his unencumbered hand sliding round to her belly. He rolls her on to her front and wrenches her on to all fours, crouching between her parted legs. Again he jerks her head back. Again she screams. The hand on her belly, levering up her vulva, is clamped across her mouth. Blood is smeared across his pubis and thighs. She convulses with fear. Flashes of light explode behind her eyes. She is suffocating. Her splayed nostrils cannot give passage to sufficient air. Her convulsions slacken and cease altogether as she loses consciousness. He takes the hand from her mouth, wrenches the head this way and that to elicit a response as his loins continue automatically to pump into her bleeding cleft.

36

I AM AN HOUR'S WALK north of Portree on the Isle of Skye, standing on cliffs overlooking the Sound of Raasay. The dark is lifting, morning coming in from the North Sea. A diagonal stab of light bisects the country, glancing across the Moray Firth, Loch Ness, Loch Oich, Loch Lochy, Loch Linnie, splitting severally at the Forth of Lorn, south and west to the Sounds of Jura and Mull. Peaks of the Grampians resolve themselves in the lifting gloom as light spreads across the country, down Glen Avon, across the Forest of Atholl, suffusing the Highlands, skipping the Inner Sound, across Raasay, glinting on the narrow strip of water between to the point of my contemplation. Behind me precipitous hills warm slowly, emerging from their charcoal twilight to tawny gorse and darker purple of the heather on their lower slopes. The sun moves on, glinting across the Sea of the Hebrides, the Little Minch, through the Sound of Harris, a silver ribbon in the looming masses of the Western Isles, diffusing in the dark waves of the Atlantic and on towards America. South of me the overlapping headlands recede in gradations of colour, each lighter than the last, disappearing in a luminous halo of sea and sky.

Some things are too beautiful to be borne.

37

THE LITTLE CABAL has broken up, the members gone their separate ways. Peter is sitting alone in his room, thinking without the stimulus of drink. The meeting has left him with the residue of two glasses of fresh orange and three cappuccinos in his mouth. He is dyspeptic. He has food for thought. He has almost reached a conclusion.

McCullen has assaulted Peter's employer and friend. McCullen is a boor. He has no friends and is particularly disliked in many quarters. More importantly, he is consciously wrecking the life of a young woman whose capacity for joy is as natural as a flower. Would this argument, he wonders, have so much force if he did not find the woman in question so attractive? Would anyone care quite as much for the mistreatment of some unlovely hag? He is sufficiently astute to realise that there is a vast prejudice in favour of the good-looking of either sex, realising also that he is not dispassionate enough to divorce himself from this.

Few would disagree that the world in general, and the Borough and Irene in particular, would be better off without McCullen. Financially, he thinks, Irene could manage. McCullen squanders in drink, other women and half a dozen dissolute pastimes almost as much money as he brings in. The welfare state would not abandon an abandoned woman. Is there somewhere in this argument a suppressed premise with Peter envisaging himself as her new benefactor? If there is he fails to admit it to himself, just as he fails to recognise the implicit chauvinism of the assumption that problems caused by a man can only be resolved through the actions of other men.

What constructive use is there in bewailing the existence of a lout and the abuses inflicted by him on his wife? None. Is it not then a logical step from desiring McCullen's non-existence to securing it? It is this point, on the brink, that Peter has reached in his ruminations. He is brooding over the abyss when Simon leaves his wife's bed.

38

IRENE IS WAKING, slowly. She senses she is lying on her back, limbs asprawl. She opens her eyes, focusing on the light till it steadies in her centre of vision. The glare from the bulb is visible through the gap of the globous shade. This was not the light she saw before losing consciousness. She remembers that he took her in the dark. She can also sense that the bed is vacant beside herself.

She attempts to move her head. A spasm of pain in her neck arrests her. She lifts her arms to cup the nape in both hands.

Her body is cold. She can feel a draught, wafting up from the soles of her feet. Somehow she knows he is not there. With an effort, elbows gaining purchase on the mattress, she levers her torso upwards.

She has been discarded lying diagonally across the bed. There is the dark swell of incipient bruising on her breast. There is blood on her thighs and on the sheet. Her face feels swollen across the lower jaw. In his leave-taking he has left every light on and every door open. The freezing draught comes from outside. Both the bedroom and front door have been left ajar. Looking downwards, between her knees, she can see Simon, standing in the hallway, regarding her with a look of limitless anguish. Oblivious to the pain, she crosses the room and slams the door, wrenching sobs as she re-crosses to the bed.

39

MCCULLEN HAS GRAVITATED towards the water and stands in the darkness, gasping on the abandoned quayside like a floundered fish. On the mud below, exposed by the receding tide, lie cans, cigarette packets, apple cores, driftwood, discarded plastic toys and whatever other detritus the river has brought with it. Like his wife an hour previously he is fighting for air, labouring, one hand on the derelict stanchion as his chest constricts.

The pace of his breathing slows. He regulates his gasps. His eyes clear from the red blur which has accumulated over the past day and evening. He looks around at the dredgings which the tides have deposited. He sees the cobbles, his feet, the unoccupied hand with a conscious self-loathing. The first flush of light has rendered the quay faintly luminous. The lapping water glows, subtly phosphorescent. He looks at the sky and is horrified by its beauty. He lets go the stanchion and stands, one hand clasping the other, palm to sweating palm, making obeisance to nothing.

There is no conscious reasoning, just the self-disgust which makes him to himself as inconsequential as the ancient pram half-submerged in the mud below. This is a new experience for McCullen who has all his life been the cynosure of his imagination. To conceive the self as worthless: he toys with the concept for a moment till he perceives this as merely another pose. And attitudes struck without an audience, he knows, are as pointless as being ironical in the path of an express train. He is annihilated. He is hollow once more. Two hours have made him friable – a man of crumbs. He is falling into dust.

He does not know he is standing in a half-crouch, body rigid, nor of the time that passes in this posture, nor of anyone who may approach. It is as if his life is seeping through the soles of his shoes into the cobbles beneath. And gradually anguish replaces the force which has ebbed from him. To feel in such a manner, he asks himself, is this reproach? And if so is there not at least a germ of hope which he has not succeeded in drowning in his beer and his whoring for so long? This is hope. If only he could have a glimpse of something other, transcendent, beyond. This is hope, the beginning of reprieve. He will suffer himself again to look at the sky and endure its ghastly beauty.

He straightens, half turning as his head twists to look over his shoulder. The exposed larynx catches the full impact as the blade swings in an arc, burying itself point-first to the hilt. McCullen lurches backwards, gargling blood, wrenching the handle from his assailant's grip. He teeters on the brink, holding one hand cupped beneath the chin in an absurd attempt to staunch the flow. The severed artery pumps great gouts of blood, down his shirt front and beyond, splashing on to the surrounding stones. His eyes cloud then instantaneously flare in the last burst of raw animal energy. One hand bracing on his face, he pulls at the knife with the other, the blade emerging with great sucking sounds. The knife tinkles on the cobbles from his bloody fingers as he moves a stride forward towards his attacker. He is sodden now and a sudden rush bursts from his nostrils also. He stands arrested, the body swaying, and falls to his knees, rocking back on his heels. He looks up, appears to want to say something. The words emerge as bloody froth. A foot is placed upon his chest; a shove which would have been merely an irritant sends him over the edge, twisting in his fall till he lands face down among the leavings, bleeding silently into the ooze – husband and wife bleeding separately.

40

THE RINGING IS insistent. She incorporates it into her dream. She surfaces from sleep unwillingly, wrapping the quilt around herself as she stumbles towards the hall. One ankle has locked and cracks with each stride as she makes for the telephone.

"Hello?"

"Carol?" It is a man's voice. She cannot readily identify the owner.

"Who is this?"

"Carol?"

Through the open door she catches sight of the luminous clock at her bedside.

"Have you no sense of time!"

"It's Irene.

"What about Irene?"

"She needs you. Go round there."

"Who is this?"

"Go round now."

"Hello . . . Hello . . . Hello . . . Christ!"

41

IT IS THE TIME of transition. Everything is in flux. The great Borough diaspora: the Glasgow fair. For two weeks factories across the conurbation shut up shop while the workforce and their families head for sunnier climes. Before easy access to the continent, these holidaymakers spread themselves for a fortnight across coastal resorts in easy reach of a paddle steamer from the Broomielaw. Small towns on the Clyde estuary resounded with noise for a fortnight. This year, McCullen has reinstated the practice. The incoming tide has detached him from his muddy bier. Face down he floats, an amorphous bundle of clothes, unnoticed among the bobbing detritus and lumps of rotting vegetation. By noon he is making fair headway down the estuary.

Irene has gone to ground. Carol is to be seen, uncharacteristically tight-lipped, shopping around the Borough, doing whatever is necessary for the care of the two she has temporarily adopted. It is the first time Irene has ever entrusted care of her children to anyone. Public opinion is divided: is Carol's unaccustomed heavy manner due to the seriousness with which she accepts her charge, or the inconvenience of altering her own holiday arrangements at such short notice? Or perhaps there is another reason. Certainly Dr Carr, on his forays to her small apartments, makes no attempt to conceal his irritation at being confronted with small children whose presence denies him his illicit copulations. The children in the lounge hear strange sounds beyond the bedroom door whose meaning they cannot fathom. There is a high-pitched sound of querulous recrimination followed by a curious pleading bleat. This is silenced by a blurred fusillade of abuse, culminating in Carol's emerging and showing him the door. It requires her mustered powers of restraint not to kick his retreating figure. She turns smilingly to the children and begins to distribute the chocolates he bought to gain admission to her loins.

Unimpeded, McCullen floats on, unmourned and unmissed. Popular speculation has it that husband and wife have jettisoned the kids for the duration of the fortnight and disappeared together in a last-ditch attempt to salvage their marriage.

Elsbeth has revived what tenuous family ties remain and gone to seek out her sister in Hull. Popular speculation regards this as a tacitly agreed and welcome rest the Frews are taking from one another. Few things here are exempt from popular speculation.

Audrey is also leaving. There is no tearing of loyalties here: she would prefer to spend her remaining weekend with her family and has invited me to Kirklee to kill two birds with one stone. We go to an early performance of a film she wants to see. I emerge disorientated in the early evening sunshine. She drives us back.

A meal is in progress with various guests. We take our places. I am, apparently, absorbed into this heterogeneous

123

group without notice. Again I am struck at their indiscriminate hospitality. Everything is plentiful except wine. All three sisters are there. Only Katrine talks. Audrey assumes the diplomatic complicity of silence. Rhys has spent her sporadic vehemence on a lately abandoned lover. The mother presides, smilingly. The talk is desultory, and she volunteers a comment rather than allow a pause to continue to daunting length. The father talks, loudly and in nervous spurts which have little bearing on the preceding topic. I am content to listen. I catch Audrey casting discreet glances twoards me across the candles, assuring herself I am not discomfited in my uncharacteristic silence.

We repair to the lounge. The father serves schnapps he has recently returned with on his travels to some academic symposium. He produces small glasses bought for the purpose and dispenses them from a little stand. I receive my measure in a glass the colour of lapis lazuli. Of the girls only Rhys is in the room. I throw the drink down my throat, feeling its welcome rasp, and go looking for the others on the pretext of finding the bathroom.

Audrey and Katrine stand with their mother in the kitchen. I can see them through the open door. They do not see me. Audrey has her hand draped carelessly across the mother's shoulders. There is an old colour supplement on the table before them which all three stare at absorbedly, standing in a shared proximity denied outsiders. There is no place in this tactile architecture for the father, or for Rhys, or for me. I feel the act of observing this frieze of love a desecration in itself. I go away.

More conversation. The guests leave. Sitting on the hall stairs with Audrey I feel a pleasing draught of night air. We walk around the garden measuring our strides on the gravel. I am assigned a room and kiss her goodnight in a house of infrequent celibacy. The other sisters customarily take their lovers with them. I lie awake and wonder what a month in America will bring.

"Three months," she tells me the following morning. I am standing in the garden, unaccustomed to the privilege in my tenement existence.

"I thought it was one."

"Three."

We go in to breakfast.

It is a timeless day. The house is bathed in light bursting through all the windows. There are more Sunday papers than can conveniently be read in a week. We dismember them, spreading the sections across the rooms. I barter a literary section from Katrine with my fashion page. The house exhales in the sunshine as we lie in the rooms quietly reading. We drink intermittent tea all afternoon.

Early evening the clouds loom. The windows are closed and curtains drawn at first dark. Audrey finishes her preparations for the following day's travel. I sit on her bed, half reading, one eye watching her deftly pack, taking pleasure from her movements and the curve of her stooping body. Her mother produces yet another meal. Katrine, the only member of the household to whom shouting comes naturally, announces dinner from the bottom of the stairwell at the top of her lungs.

We eat in silence. Audrey is leaving early the following morning, catching her connecting flight from London. I think it polite to leave early and excuse myself from the table to gather my things. When I return Audrey is regaling the others with impersonations of cartoon characters which cease abruptly the moment I enter the room. They all turn as if expecting an explanation of my presence.

"Don't let me interrupt . . ." Indulgent smiles all round

but still no one continues. "I'm looking for a railway timetable for Glasgow Central."

Audrey stands and I follow her into the next room. It is a reduced Sunday service. I will have to travel to Johnstone and board there. I find myself suddenly incapable of reading a timetable or of folding the sheet once I know the time of my train.

Audrey will drive me to the station. They are still sitting round the remains of the meal when I take my leave. The father nods at my retreating body. I do not think he knows who I am. The others speak their farewells and I think: "They are very civil, but he does not know my name, and beside Katrine they do not care if they never see me again."

It is dark when we make it to the car and rain slants through the headlights. She nudges the car cautiously to the road outside. Wipers clear the screen in rhythmic sweeps. Her driving, like everything else done in my company, is cautious. I glance at her in the glow of the passing lamp lights. Her gaze is fixed ahead.

The street lights disappear as we leave the village. I can feel her concentration on the dark gap to Johnstone. At the first lights of the approaching small town she allows herself a sideways smile. There is no question of conversation. We negotiate a bend and are presented fleetingly with the spectacle of a dog which has run on to the road and stands nonplussed in the glare of our lights. She does well to swerve, but I can feel the jolt of bone against the wheel arch on my side. A hundred feet on she has stopped us dead and is rigidly clutching the steering wheel.

I open the door and run back. In the half-light I can see the dog, an aged bitch, half-beagle, with rows of teats. She lies in the centre of the road having ricocheted off the high kerb. She is vulnerable now to traffic from both lanes.

Running towards her and opposite me is a young man in denims. She makes an attempt to stand and flounders clumsily. I am almost at her when another car rounds the corner at speed. The bitch is taken between the wheels. I hear her glance on the underside of the chassis. The driver accelerates away; the young man who is now level with me pursues the retreating tail lights shouting "Bastard! Bastard!"

The bitch rolls half a dozen times and flops on her forepaws, curiously alert. Her hind legs slump uselessly. I am frightened as I approach, half expecting her to be burst on the side concealed from me, leaking guts. How can I kill her quickly if she is in pain? An aged bitch, gone in the mouth and mangled. I am more frightened still as I stoop to examine.

There are no obvious lesions. I am hesitant to pick her up and compound some internal rupture, but can't let her lie in the middle of the road. As I gather her up she makes no noise. I lift her, her back cradled along the length of my forearms. Her eyes are black. The young man returns and walks with me to the kerb, examining the dog as we go. We stand hunched, conferring in the rain.

"There's a police station there." I can see the sign, looking in the direction of his nod. "Do you want to make a cradle with your arms and mine and we'll carry her."

"No need. She's not heavy. I've a car." I also nod. He follows me several yards, a few paces behind, making solicitous sounds. I have no idea if they are intended for the dog or me. She still lies still.

"If you're sure there's nothing else . . ."

"There's honestly nothing you can do."

He shrugs his shoulders. His face is hard and open and honest. It obviously goes against the grain, abandoning dogs or children or women. Perhaps he is always first there. I watch him turn and walk off in the rain.

Audrey still sits in the posture in which I left her, hunched forward, hands clasping the wheel tightly. I clamber in, saying "It's all right, it's all right, it's all right," with no idea whether I'm speaking to the bitch or Audrey or myself. She also has seen the police station, indicates and cranks the car forward. The dog, galvanised by the motion, flexes herself and rolls on to the car floor. She sits without obvious discomfort.

I pat her, making what I imagine to be soothing noises. We take less than a minute to arrive. As I open the door the bitch jumps out and awaits me on the kerb expectantly, obviously revived. I am unprepared for this and carry her into the police station to corroborate my story of a concussed animal. They listen and seem to find nothing remarkable in what I say. The desk sergeant passes me a piece of string, one end of which I loop round her collar, the other passed through the hinged recess beneath the counter. He leads her through. She is happy to oblige and stands contentedly as he ties the string to a desk leg, ordering a subordinate to fetch her a biscuit and some water.

I am handed a form. Remembering my train I scribble some perfunctory details and shout thanks over my shoulder. The engine turns over as I emerge. We move forward as soon as I am seated beside her.

I feel expected to make conversation but have no idea what to say. The incident with the dog and our imminent separation has left me anxious and confused. She slows at the approach of the station as we splash into the small car park. The waiting room lights are on and condensation has formed on the inside of the windows. The track runs straight in either direction, dwindling into the darkness.

There is no sign of the train's approach. We have at least several minutes. I wonder is she is similarly anxious. I think: "She is young and she is going to a strange place. No matter what it is like she will see something exotic in it. She will meet other people – other men. No matter what they are like she will find something exotic in them. She is young and she is almost beautiful. Three months is a long time, at such an age, with such an appearance, in such a place. If she wants to go give her the opportunity now. Do not spend three months loving against the law of diminishing returns."

And I said to her: "I would like still to be with you when you come back. If you will wait, I will too. Will you wait?"

She nods her head and her mouth forms the word "yes". She makes no sound. Not knowing what else to do I kiss her face, pressing my lips hard against her. Her seatbelt encumbers me. Why is it, I wonder, that at my most traumatic I often experience a sense of my own ridiculousness?

"Don't stay here. It's minutes yet. I hate goodbyes. Please write."

"Yes."

I leave the car, crossing to the ticket office, fumbling my change under the guichet. At my back I can hear the engine again engage. I walk back to wave goodbye but she has already checked the rear-view mirror and does not see. I stand with my hand above my head until the car is out of sight.

I am the only one on the platform waiting in the open. The others huddle in the crush of the waiting room. A light appears in the distance at the point where the lines appear to converge. The train thunders in in a wave of turbulence. The doors open with a pneumatic hiss. The other passengers scurry forward from the waiting room, arranging themselves in ragged groups round the open doors. I wait until the congestion clears. My hair can absorb no more. Water trickles down the front of my face as I step into the light and hear the doors close at my back. I experience a feeling of being shut in or shut out. I don't know which.

42

IRENE HAS SURFACED and McCullen has sunk. A week of maceration ended his nautical career when the bloated relic of what had once been a man bumped to a standstill in the quiet shallows. After this it is merely a matter of time. Local children habitually beachcomb, dredging the shallows for rubbish jettisoned upstream.

Some small boys wade purposefully through the water, turning over with sticks anything which attracts their curiosity. They approach the bundle of McCullen and stop. They confer. Three come closer and stop. They exchange apprehensive glances. One, demonstrating more temerity than his fellows, comes closer still, poking with a stick the reptilian sac of McCullen's inflated leather jacket. As yet his mind has not identified the floating bundle. A deft flick and the corpse turns turtle. McCullen exhales a putrescent lungful of air and settles gracefully, his face six inches beneath the surface. The children disperse to the points of the compass, gathering together later to corroborate alibis of their whereabouts – elsewhere. Half an hour later a middle-aged woman on the tow path is presented with the spectacle of a dough-coloured man sunbathing beneath the water. A frenzied telephone call summons two uniformed men who reconnoitre and them summon others. Dying is a largely administrative affair. McCullen has effortlessly generated paperwork. He is lifted on to a tarpaulin and wrapped gingerly in plastic cerements, lest he fall apart like sodden cheese. The headmaster is using syllogisms on the hapless truants.

"One body cannot be in two places at the same time. Correct?"

"Yes, sir." In ragged chorus.

"All of you claim that you were somewhere else at the same time. Correct?"

"Yes, sir."

"You have been telling untruths."

"Yes, sir."

"Serious offences merit serious punishments."

"Yes, sir."

"Lying is a serious offence."

"Yes, sir."

"'Untruth' is a synonym for lying."

They turn to the boy who poked the corpse.

"It's a fair cop, sir."

"You have been watching too much television."

"Yes, sir."

"Television blunts the moral sense."

"Yes, sir."

"This requires correction."

". . . Yes, sir."

"The word 'correction' is derived from the Latin 'corrigere', meaning, roughly, to rule."

This sounds like a specious etymology working up to a point. They are at a loss.

"Really, sir."

"Pass me my rule."

The headmaster is gleefully beating the truants as McCullen, encased in plastic, returns in the direction from which he has just come.

Irene's reappearance in the Borough precedes news of the corpse by several hours. She is to be seen, conversing grim-faced with Carol, sitting at the latter's lounge window. She is there when the police arrive at her untenanted house, and still there as the methodical sweep widens. News of their presence reaches her before they do. She again leaves the children and finds the constable standing stolidly at the close entrance. He is reticent to answer her questions and suggests they go inside. She is insistent. The distance is too great, their voices pitched too low: neighbours across the way are tantalised by the mime. They see the constable speak into his radio, and minutes later are rewarded by the sight of an unmarked car rounding the corner. Two men emerge wearing coats. Jehovah's Witnesses are unlikely in the Borough. Another exchange ensues while Irene obstinately refuses to budge from the doorstep. The rising cadence of her voice is hovering on the verge of comprehensibility when one of the men says something which silences her. She stands stoically for several seconds while the three men scrutinise her reaction as closely as her neighbours. Half a minute later she is fumbling with her keys while she stumbles in the gloom of the tenement corridor. The constable remains while the two men follow.

They await her in the lounge while she prepares tea. At such a time the niceties must be maintained. She pours with remarkable composure. They apologise for the inconvenience of their questions at such a time. Procedure is specific. She sips with her eyes closed and accepts the situation with a nod. Their questions are meticulous. They are patient, noting each answer and the time taken to deliver it.

Now that she has taken off her scarf they see her collar. Is anything wrong? Whiplash. The result of a car accident then? Yes, a car accident. Were other vehicles involved? Yes – no. There were no other vehicles involved. It was an emergency stop. She was driving then? Yes. Does she possess a car? Would she be living in a place like this if she could afford a car? A friend's perhaps? A friend of a friend's. A very obliging friend of a friend, one of them comments. Very obliging, she replies. She visited a casualty unit then? She had the collar as the result of a previous accident and felt it would help. No visits to the hospital then? No visits she confirms.

A woman police constable arrives, observes the situation and hovers deferentially in the hallway. The men finish what they stress to be their preliminary enquiries and take their leave. The woman constable sees them to the door, returning to the room to find Irene sitting with her head in her hands.

43

A CURIOUS SILENCE had settled on the Borough sub-Post Office. I thought it was merely Elsbeth who was in the shop at my arrival. She handed a packet of sandwiches to Simon and regarded me with a blank expression. But it was not Elsbeth. She sensed something of an unusual tension and was curious enough to pause for several moments, looking for an excuse to remain longer. Finding none she left. We all watched her walk out.

I turned round, expecting the expressions to lighten. I

had no reason for being there beyond the desire to see my friends. After a few commonplaces I too felt the need for a pretext, and began to pretend to be interested in some picture postcards. A few more sallies and still neither of them would rally. Nor would they admit to anything being wrong. Peter was pretending to be carrying out a stock check. It was the first time I had seen them looking awkward in that small space, squeezing past while feet apart, observing an inviolable body space which the interior wouldn't allow. They were cautious in their eye movements also, looking directly at me but not at one another.

"What price conversation? The century is drawing to its close." Mumbled replies. I took my leave and followed Elsbeth. Peter caught me up a hundred yards from the shop as I walked in the direction of town. He was struggling with his jacket, the coordination of fitting arms in sleeves while negotiating the traffic beyond him. After the hush of the Post Office he spoke in shouts. Simon, watching him go, retrieved the sandwiches from the bin and began mechanically to chew.

"Where are you going?"

"There's no need to shout. And what was all that about?"

"What?"

"The Rue Morgue back there. Neither of you were murdered and there's no love lost on McCullen."

"True."

"So why the atmosphere?"

"Sometimes things get that way. Y'know."

"No."

"So where are you going?" I knew the question was a refusal to elaborate.

"Into town." There was insufficient time for him to walk

with me and be back before the end of lunch. I could see his eyes swivel to the bars.

"Fancy a drink?"

"It's too early. Why must all your social occupations revolve around alcohol?"

"Fuck you."

"Walk me as far as the café. We could take a sandwich out on the grass for half an hour." The invitation took the sting out of him. It took him another hundred yards to get his jacket on.

"How's your doctor woman? What's her name – Angela?"

"Audrey."

"Yes . . . her . . ."

"Fine."

"America isn't it – she's gone to I mean."

"Yes."

"New Orleans?"

"New York."

"Yes. New York. You told me . . . The Big Easy."

"The Big Apple."

"Yes . . . Has she written?"

"No."

"Still – Y'know how it is. New place, new things . . ."

"Yes."

"Yes. I expect she's got lots on her mind."

"I expect so."

"Different way of life, so I'm told . . ."

"Yes," I said. It didn't matter what I said, he wasn't talking to anyone besides himself. I could see he was thinking frantically beneath his agitated monologue. We bought long Vienna rolls with salad fillings and a carton of milk each. He wouldn't even sit down to eat but stood with one foot tapping, chewing with as little relish as Simon, or walked up and down talking about nothing while the mayonnaise oozed down his shirt front. I gave him a chance to finish and hoped he might come out with the reason for the tension at work. He ceased abruptly in mid-sentence, threw the uneaten half into a bin, pretended to look at his watch and left with the pretence of duty calling. I watched him go by the route which would take him past the pub he wanted to go into in the first place. I finished my lunch, fed his to the birds and left.

44

I AM STANDING at the window, thinking. I spend too much time thinking. It is the brief metropolitan twilight. What time is it in America? What is the point in such speculations? At that moment I think it better to live a life of tangential distractions. At that moment the telephone rings.

"You know the one call they give you in the films? This is it." It is Peter. There is a false bravado in the voice and I can sense his fear.

"Where are you?"

"The police station." It is two minutes off the Borough High Street. I tell him I will be there in five.

"No. Not there. I went there first but they took me in to town."

They have taken him to the main station of the city. I tell him I will be there in half an hour and to say nothing further till my arrival. "We've signed the Geneva Convention haven't we?" he asks before I hang up.

I take a taxi and pay the hackney, rattling in the darkness, before entering the police station. After a brief discussion with the sergeant I am shown into a room where the two men in mufti who interviewed Irene sit smoking cigarettes. They look singularly unamused and tired. One is unshaven. They have a weary air of insufficient sleep. The room is bare besides the deal table and moulded chairs. One has an open notepad before him.

"You the one he 'phoned?'

"Yes." I tell them my name. The one who has not yet spoken nods to his companion. I have already been questioned in their routine enquiries.

"I don't suppose you can account for your friend's whereabouts the other night?" They have hazarded a guess at the time of death. The question has already been asked dozens of times round the Borough.

"No." This is consistent with what I had told them before. Perhaps it gratifies them that I do not trump up some false corroboration. Perhaps it is what they wanted to hear. The one who is not smoking and who has not yet spoken stands up.

"Do you want a cup of tea?"

"Please." He leaves the room. The other scrapes back a chair for me. I seem to have been incorporated into the air of weary camaraderie. I sit. There is a brief silence.

"Do you know him well?"

"Yes."

"And what type of person does he strike you as?"

The plainclothes officer appears with a tray. There are three cups and a plate of nondescript biscuits. In the distribution I am given time to weigh my answer.

"Precipitate."

"What?" They exchange a tired smile. "It doesn't do to take down statements of someone wordy. No one's writing but keep it simple."

"He's rash." And after a pause, "he's young." This appears to agree with their own conclusions. "What's he supposed to have done?"

"He says he murdered someone."

There is a pause while I consider the absurdity of his statement. They are patient in awaiting a reaction. Involuntarily I burst out laughing. When I begin to subside I think of Peter and his incongruity in a place like this, sweating in a solitary cell for his fictitious crimes. This again starts me. The room reverberates hollowly. When at last I cease they are still patiently waiting.

"And you take him seriously?"

"Someone is dead, killed by person or persons unknown. We have to take statements like that seriously. Even from people like your friend, if only to eliminate them as a possibility."

"He's incapable of such an act."

"You seem sure of that."

"Yes. You must have seen enough murdered people and their murderers to know."

"You'd be surprised. Most murders occur in domestic circumstances."

"He lives alone. Does he look to you like someone who could kill another person?" Again they exchange glances. They seem quite unperturbed by my reversal of roles. "I know as much as anyone else in the Borough who reads the local rag. McCullen was found way down the estuary. Chances are he was killed nearer home. Perhaps you know where. Even if you don't, if you haven't got a location or a suspect, your autopsy would give you a method. As far as I know that's been kept confidential. Did Peter corroborate what you already know?"

They make no reply. I take this for tacit consent.

"Well then. For goodness sake . . ."

"What other friends does he have besides yourself?"

"There's several of us often drink together."

"And those nearer his own age?"

"Not so often any more."

"And women?"

"I don't understand. Even if you suspect him of having an accomplice, is it likely to be a woman?"

"Perhaps. It's also plausible that he concocted his story to cover someone else, who may or may not be a woman."

That shook me.

"So far we've had three confessions, two from confirmed cranks who have confessed to everything from the sinking of the Titanic on. Your friend doesn't conveniently fit that category. These people are habitual and renowned. And most often they're solitary people who confess for the sake of eight hours' company. The possibility of being sent down is an added bonus. That's not the case with your friend. Did he often keep the company of women?"

"On and off. As far as I know there's been no one recently. It's more the kind of thing he'd keep to himself."

"Did he know Mrs McCullen?"

"It's the Borough. Everyone knows everyone."

"Did he ever keep company with Mrs McCullen?"

"No more than me or anyone else for that matter."

"Was she one of the group of friends you talked about."

"Peripherally," I catch myself. "She was on the border. I've had her round to mine with friends. It's not that she's any less friendly, it's just that it was hard for her, married to a man like McCullen."

"Your friend we're holding next door, was he one of the people you had round at the same time as Mrs McCullen?"

"Yes."

"And did he appear to pay her particular attention?"

"No more than being sociable demanded."

"Was Mr McCullen there?"

"No one entertained Mr McCullen. He was too volatile ever to invite anywhere."

"You say things were socially difficult for Mrs McCullen, having the husband she did."

"Yes."

"Would people have paid her more attention, socially I mean, if she hadn't been married to McCullen?"

"No doubt. She's very attractive and she's young. She's easy to like."

"What do you think your friend's attitude to her would be if she was unattached?"

"Who know? That's impossible to say. As I said, she's attractive."

"He never discussed such a possibility?"

"Not that I can remember."

"Is there anyone you know whose behaviour towards her would markedly change if she suddenly found herself unattached?"

"No," I lied.

The conversation had taken a turn I didn't like. It drifted on until they realised they'd get nothing further from my non-committal replies.

"Take your friend away and make sure he doesn't show his face at a station again. We've already impressed that on him."

They certainly had. They escorted him to the area where I was waiting. He was cowed. I affected levity till the taxi I hailed drew up. We were still within sight of the station and I knew they would be watching.

"Get in," I said, between my teeth. He was completely docile.

45

I HAVE JUST FINISHED lunch with Katrine and left her at the Underground. She is going home. She will take a tube and a train to Kirklee. We talked about her course. She is reading history. At my prompting she fished several of the texts she is studying from her bag and read aloud some extracts. I hadn't the heart to tell her. The people these passages described would have died laughing at the sensibilities of those who wrote them, their need for concealment, of abattoirs and conduits dripping unseen shit inside house walls. I've lived in places where they killed the livestock in the garden till the soil was black with blood. Pieces like that could have been written by Henry Carr.

Although I was burning with curiosity I let her bring up the topic of Audrey. She has telephoned home. It appears that she is too busy to be lonely and has met some artists. I could have found out for myself. Distance is no obstacle. To do so strikes me as tantamount to reading someone's diary. If she wants to tell me she will.

We talked desultorily of other things too. I could tell by the cadence of her sentences that the conversation had drawn to a close. When the waitress removed the plates we had no reason to stay. I kissed her off at the tube and watched her walk carelessly away, pretty, erect, unconsciously carrying all the favourable ratios, buoyed by a kind of ecstatic suspension.

46

DETECTIVE INSPECTOR Thomson has explained to me that most murders stem from domestic incidents and occur in domestic circumstances. This, he told me, is why inquiries begin from the home circle and radiate outwards. Aside from this, the majority of police work involves routine investigation in an attempt to establish patterns. Patterns of crimes with the same *modus operandi*, in the same location, in chronological order, for the same motive, upon victims of the same social standing, or of a similar hair colour, who may or may not visit the same launderette. In short, any conceivable and many implausible patterns. And if a suspect falls conveniently into one of these patterns it tends to substantiate the method of investigation. And if a suspect falls into two, he or she is likely to get a lot of police attention.

There are the odd exceptions: the crime of passion that flares from incandescent love a weekend old. Were someone, bearing no relation to the victim, to walk up to a doorstep and slaughter the householder without provocation, then unless apprehended in the act there is little likelihood of his or her being caught. With this in mind the two policemen I talked with in the interview room and their colleagues have questioned the locals minutely on anything untoward which may have occurred in the Borough, of anything even remotely out of the ordinary, of anything or anyone, sir or madam, conspicuous in the least degree . . .

Comparing notes they had cobbled together a description of the man they would like to interview to help them with their inquiries: he is small, early middle-aged, tonsured, running to fat and is armed with hornrimmed spectacles and a bunch of drooping violets.

Two nights later a man resembling this description is found loitering lugubriously outside a tenement block. Dragged, expostulating, into the station, he invokes every name from the Home Secretary to the Chief Constable and all influential colleagues in promising reprisals for this ignominy. The Duty Sergeant, an aged veteran with a flare for monotone rebuttals, appraises the figure before him at a glance and silences the tirade with: "Certainly sir, we will return the prophylactics with the rest of your effects as soon as the Principal arrives." If nothing else, apprehended on another of his pornographic forays, Henry Carr has provided them with an amusing diversion.

But there is still the need to eliminate him from their list of suspects. Henry's reticence to reveal his whereabouts on certain nights is, he assures them, not because he does not appreciate the gravity of the situation. "An *affaire de coeur*," he says, "the oldest and most understandable transgression."

But they are not as understanding as he hopes. They want something concrete and impress this upon him to such a degree that within half an hour he is blurting out tearful admissions that leave the vice squad dazed by his ingenuity. But he is not the stuff of which murderers are made. They know this before corroboration of his whereabouts is obtained and the investigation grinds purposelessly on.

47

"Maybe." She can only glimpse them sectioned by the chink in the door, extended as wide as the restraining chain allows.

"Miss Carol Elder?"

There is no Christian name on the plate outside. For the moment the significance of the fact escapes her.

"Those coats are a dead give-away," she says.

"Sorry?"

"The last *Watchtower* you left me was laid out for my cat to shit on."

"We're policemen." They provide identification. An interview is inevitable.

"Come in."

They refuse to take off their coats and sit sweltering in her tropical lounge. Her idea of etiquette demands tea regardless.

"Miss Elder, when the constable questioned you in our door-to-door inquiries you told him that you spent some time with Mrs McCullen."

"Yes."

"And you confirmed that you were with her on the night we were particularly interested in."

"So?"

"A Dr Henry Carr has informed us otherwise."

"The little shit!"

48

THREE LAPS OF THE Borough: Peter has walked three times round the circumference of his world and, in his present state, found it wanting. Leaving me with a gruff disclaimer, he departed our taxi and vanished into the night. I was inquisitive enough to visit the Post Office the following morning and found Simon alone, eyeing me expectantly. I knew he knew nothing of the phone call and Peter's reprieve of the previous night, but he knew I knew something he did not. On the few occasions Peter has not shown, one of us has gone to his lodgings to shake him from drunken sleep. I volunteered and ambled round, knowing in advance I would find his bed empty. He had made a meal of sorts, fairly recently, but the bed was cold as stone. Rather than face Simon's concerned questions, I telephoned a lie across and allowed the pips to overtake me, hanging up on the excuse of no more change. I thought of looking for Peter but thought better of it. Tomorrow was the weekend – he was confused enough to be allowed to asphyxiate for two more days before being brought round.

On completing his third circuit he turns and looks inwards, to the Borough lights in the growing dark. He has eaten without hunger or relish. His pockets are full of money, which, for some reason, he provided himself with before walking into the police station, stocking up for his incarceration. Moderately solvent and in a state of complete vacuity he turns his steps towards town.

He finds her quite by chance, sitting on a barstool on the edge of her group and with an air of complete self-reliance curiously at odds with that of her companions. In a state of paralysed sobriety which normally precludes any social intercourse with women, he draws up a stool unnecessarily close, slaps the bar and orders a beer with the whimsical extravagance of Don Quixote. Catching the barman's eye at the tap, she doubles the order by extending two slim fingers and pays for both in a fluid movement, sliding several notes across the bar. The change is waved away in a gesture of equal extravagance. Peter accepts his drink with puzzled gratitude and turns to appraise her with the blatant scrutiny she has levelled upon him.

She is of middling height with shoulder-length brown hair, pale skin and a pleasing figure which her clothes are worn to accentuate. She is obviously accustomed to being looked at. They start at the ankles, taking silent inventory of one another and not till he reaches her eyes does he realise what is remarkable in her: despite her attitude of intelligence they are as vacuous as his own. It is a reciprocal acknowledgement, realised at the same instant. They taste their beers in concert, and, knowing it will do nothing to slake their thirsts, simultaneously stand. His hand rises to take her extending arm. With her free hand she picks up her bag. They walk out of the bar and into the fortuitous taxi which he flags down.

They sit at either end of the cab, looking at each other in the darkness without touching. He has to be roused from this preoccupation to give his address. She enters his bedsit first, assumes the interior at a glance, stands in the centre of the room and takes off her dress before the door has closed. Without a word he kneels in front of her and begins tearing at her tights. She strains against him, affording purchase, seizes his hair, tilts his head towards her and bites his lip till it bleeds. He smears the blood on her navel. She raises herself on the balls of her feet, burying his face in her pudenda. He pulls his clothes off also. She spits in his hair and pulls him down. They fuse with a seismic shudder which shocks them both by its vehemence.

The temporary exhaustion serves only to whet their appetites. Several times they lock and strain against one another in erotic conflict. They lose all track of time. Several times one of them falls into a narcotic sleep only to be roused by the insistent demands of the other. He dresses and goes to the communal kitchen, bringing back some salami, cheeses and whatever meagre provisions remain. She eats ravenously while he undresses. When he is naked they look at one another, ignore the food and feast on their sex, coupling frenziedly among the broken crackers. For the parched aftermath of their fucking he brings jugs of water which do not slake their thirsts either.

She dons some clothes, walks into the hall and orders a taxi on the pay phone. Thinking she intends to leave alone he grasps her when she walks back into the room, pulling her towards the yet unused bed. She asks him to dress and says they are going to hers. The horn sounds before he has time to put on socks. He pulls canvas shoes on over bare feet. When they emerge it is barely dark, whether dawn or dusk he does not know.

Her place is better than his, larger, self-contained, better appointed. She closes all the curtains, eschews the bedroom, grappling with him in the lounge. He marvels at her gifts of erotic improvisation. She knows he makes up in the fluid candour of his actions what he lacks in experience. Their love-making is violent and intermittent. For the first time they sleep simultaneously, lying on the hearthrug with the duvet from the single bed.

He sleeps a hundred years and wakes to find her spooning tapioca into her mouth from a ragged tin. She has provided food. There is fruit scattered on the floor between them. He eats sardines, and cheese, tears lumps of wheaten bread from their loaf and shares her dessert. They drink bottles of bitter German lager. She walks to the bathroom and reappears having rouged her nipples. He licks jam from her thighs. She tongues pitted olives into his mouth and smears chocolate on his belly. Again and again they lock with a compulsive desperation that will not subside.

For periods whose length he cannot calculate he lies looking lethargically at the ceiling. He can hear her walking from room to room without purpose. Roused again he goes hunting and finds her lying on the kitchen linoleum, legs apart, expectant. Afterwards they resume their vigil, without curiosity.

He sleeps for another century and wakes to find her beside him on the hearthrug, curled vulnerably. She wakes to find him pulling on his clothes. When questioned he says he needs some air. Both know any departure will ruin their hermetic orgy. She bars his way. He ducks under her restraining arm. The open door sucks out the foetid cloud of their heavy sex.

He makes the street to find the sky luminous with the radiance of first light. The neighbourhood is alien but he remembers the small park at the end of the road where other roads converge. He can see the dark foliage from where he stands. As he begins to walk he can hear the door slam behind him. He reaches the wrought-iron fence as the sound of slapping footfalls catches up: she has come without shoes. They regard each other for an instant. He offers cupped hands to help her over the low barrier. She is slender enough to squeeze past a missing stanchion. Without fatigue he vaults the fence.

The park is little more than an acre of trampled byways and tenacious shrubs. Occasional trees ring the outside and sprout randomly across the square. They are standing in a sink of mud. He looks at her feet and kisses her lips hard. She pulls off what clothes she wears. He follows suit. She puts her arms around his neck. He braces. She takes her weight, raising and splaying her legs. He feels the chill of her crossed calves against his buttocks. He takes her standing, kneeling finally in the mud with their combined weight. He rolls her on her back, pushing insistently till, in a mutual blur, she screams, a strange animal ululation in the climax of their pleasure. He slumps on her, both gasping in the ooze like landed fish.

It is several minutes before he can coordinate his movements to dress. She precedes him and walks to the point where they entered. He climbs wearily over the fence as she again slips through. In the half-light they regard one another, knowing it is over. Neither know the other's surname. She lifts her hand and touches his cheek in the first gesture of tenderness that either of them have expressed since their meeting. As they separate he can hear the sucking noise of her feet on the moist morning pavement. With a stab of reproach he realises he did not return her parting courtesy.

He makes Kelvingrove at the first stirring of people abroad. The first bench he reaches is occupied by a sleeping vagrant, mouth agape. At the next seat he slumps in exhausted dejection, sitting motionless for several hours as the city awakens. He contemplates buying a Sunday supplement and returning to the bench with which he feels a closer affinity than his room. But, he realises, he has no socks, no money – which is left at his lodgings or sunk in the mud – and no prospects.

His reverie is interrupted by a crocodile of schoolchildren, small uniformed girls from the private establishment of Park Circus, led in single file to assimilate the cultural heritage of Sam, the Bengal tiger who died in the Calderpark Zoo in 1964. Somewhere in his debauch he has lost a day.

The disorientation is staggering. Nor has he done what he set out to. He stumbles towards his lodgings and stops short in the main street, a hundred yards from the Post Office. There are available detours; he does not need to pass his workplace. Again he takes stock and walks resolutely forward, losing confidence at the door, stepping inside almost furtively. His loins sting; his feet are filthy; underneath his clothes he is coated in mud and sperm and grass and chocolate and vulval smearings. Emerging from the back kitchen with a cup of tea Simon catches sight of the prodigal. They stand looking at one another for several minutes till Simon steps forward to proffer the steaming mug. Peter accepts, leaning heavily on the periodicals in quiet gratitude, doing all in his power to stifle a convulsive sob.

49

"YOU LIED OVER THE 'phone then?"

"Yes."

"He wasn't there at all?"

"Yes."

"Yes he was or yes he wasn't?"

"Yes he wasn't."

I muttered something about means and ends and ordered two more beers. Peter, miraculously, hadn't come with us to the pub. Simon had dispatched him to bed after he had fallen asleep over the postal orders. It was the first time in an age we had gone drinking without him.

"Where was he then?"

"You described the state he was in to me. Work it out for yourself."

"It's difficult to imagine what you would have to do to get in a state like that."

"Try."

"It wasn't just the filth and the tiredness. I think he was terribly upset. Do you think he was upset?"

"Yes."

"Yes . . . so do I. And when I mentioned that the police were still in the area he went pale. Do you think he's in trouble?"

"Did he say anything?" I asked.

"About what?"

"About the police?"

"Yes, curiously enough . . ." he tailed off, withdrawing again into his own private speculation.

"Do I get this in instalments? Perhaps you'd like me to come back next week?"

"No – sorry. When I mentioned the police he said we'd have to talk but not just now because he was too tired. And when I said I was seeing you for a drink he said he gave you *carte blanche*."

"No he didn't." I knew Peter had never used an expression like that in his life.

"I'm paraphrasing of course."

"You've been reading the *Reader's Digest* word quiz again, haven't you?" I'd attempted to steer the conversation off but this time the gambit didn't work. Again he knew I knew something he didn't. This time he wasn't prepared to let the topic lapse.

"If this is something to do with Peter and he has said he doesn't mind your telling me, have you any right to keep it to yourself?"

"That's not fair. If he wants you to know, why not tell you himself? Why foist the job on me?" They were neither of them questions. "Besides, I feel personally compromised."

"You're lying again, aren't you?"

"Yes," I said.

"As far as you're concerned he can tell me everything?"

"That's up to him."

"And you give him *carte blanche*?"

"If he knows what it means."

"That's big of you. You tell me he can tell all and then you sneer at his lack of words."

"He won't need many. And I'm not sneering. I'm his friend."

"Really? And you won't mention as a favour something he's too embarrassed to talk about himself."

We sat in silence as I thought for a moment.

"Do you have a cigarette?"

"Neither of us smoke," he said.

"Peter presented himself at the police station early Thursday night and confessed to McCullen's murder. One look at him and they knew. They've seen enough murderers. And nothing he said corroborated any of the known facts. He called me and we left together. I wanted to shout at him but hadn't the heart. I've never seen him that dejected."

"Was he drunk?"

"He was intoxicated."

"Have you any idea why he did such a thing?"

"They think he may be trying to cover for someone else."

"Why?"

"Perhaps the oldest reason: love. With Peter, who knows. A Quixotic notion of chivalry. Perhaps he thought he was getting a real stab at altruism for the first time in his life. And he couldn't even get that right."

"Who do they think he was trying to cover for?"

"They don't know. They think in all probability a woman." His face became quite a study when I said that. I could practically see him calculate all the permutations until his reasoning arrived at the wrong conclusion.

"Do you think it was real love or, just as you say," he gave a vague wave, "chivalry?"

"As I said, he was intoxicated. Drunk on his own decency. He's got a remarkable gift of doing the wrong things for the right reasons."

"Even if he loves her, I won't have anyone shoulder my burdens. Do you . . ." it was barely a whisper, "do you think he loves her?"

"No. I think in one respect the police were all wrong. I don't think he thought he was covering for a woman. I think he thought he was covering for a man. For you. I think he loves you."

50

A CURIOUS THING HAS happened to Simon since our discussion. A change has overcome him: he is subtly illuminated. If any have noticed, few have mentioned. The change has affected Peter too, if only because he unconsciously imbibes all that is given him by his employer. A seed, given the night of my disclosure, has germinated.

As usual, nothing in the outward aspect of Simon is affected. Nor have his feelings towards Irene suffered any diminution because he has found something commensurate with his capacity for love. If anything, Peter has occupied the space in his affections vacated by Elsbeth when she decamped from his heart with the overpriced parcel to Nairobi. The air of sad resignation which he evinced towards Irene, changed to tepid hope at her husband's death, is unaltered.

Neither of us told Peter of our discussion. He is too embarrassed to enquire. A few days after his absence he drew Simon aside.

"This has nothing to do with what happened . . . recently. I feel as if I'm not doing anything here. There's nothing wrong with the job, don't think that. But I feel it's like I'm sinking in jam." An image of her thighs a week previously, smeared with blackcurrant preserve, floats into his mind. His loins give a reflex tingle.

"You're stultifying," said Simon. It is the word which has been hanging over his own life since his conscription into the sub-Post Office.

"Yes. I must go."

"Of course you must. Give me some notice when you've finally decided and I'll find a replacement." The love of the son he never had is enough. He would not fetter the boy. Peter is taken aback by this easy acquiescence. He had been prepared for recriminations.

"Right." Now that his absence is on the agenda he feels no sudden inclination to move. The atmosphere of late has been very congenial.

There is another curious aspect to this turn of events.

Since the recently advertised trip to her sister's home, Elsbeth has addressed a steady stream of letters to Hull. This attempt to re-establish family links, both parents being long since dead, has coincided with a slackening of her Presbyterian zeal. The coffee mornings and the church bazaars have been allowed to lapse while she sits in her cold bedroom scribbling furtive sentiments on her headed lavender notepaper. In other aspects also her behaviour has been decidedly odd.

She has taken to insomniac wanderings while Simon sleeps soundly. Each morning she anxiously scans the mail, throwing aside with irritation the promotional circulars. No mail has arrived postmarked from England: Simon concludes that this is a one-sided sorority. Her attitude towards him has also changed. She has re-established the habit of providing him with sandwiches, which she insists on delivering and he continues secretly to jettison. Perhaps she has noticed the ambience of his workplace. A cooked meal awaits him every week night, replacing the cold collations between plates and the cursory note explaining her whereabouts. There have even been occasional bottles of wine: bloody burgundy to complement the stew. Simon is bemused. They remain uncommunicative. These unexplained offerings are the only redress her reticent soul is capable of. It is as if by exhibiting the symptoms she is attempting to elicit the condition. And the presupposition of Simon's perpetual affection, which she could revive at her convenience, has been exploded. She is dismayed to find her niche in his heart usurped. She does not know by whom. She now sleeps next to a man who goes through the motions of married life with no more care for her than his kindly nature would extend towards a stray cat. She is astute enough to realise that these propitiatory concessions will not animate a love that perished for want of recognition, and she lacks the magnanimity to come clean.

I notice she condescends to walk the Borough streets more frequently than before. And she appears to be dragging something. Her reputation precedes her: people are hesitant in saying hello lest they receive a snub. She travels in a pocket of silence of her own making. Her recent attentions towards Simon are an attempt to pierce the membrane. She is not in love. She is lonely.

"Simon."

"Yes?"

"I think I'll visit my sister soon."

"Again?"

"Yes." She is waiting for him to remonstrate.

"As you like."

51

"ASHES TO ASHES, dust to dust . . ." and a hastily muttered valediction in the vaguest of terms. It is difficult to reconcile the memory with the compliments. The priest gallantly continues, aware that the few who attend the graveside do so merely out of a sense of propriety, or in deference to Irene. It is even rumoured that a few are present to ensure McCullen is permanently dead.

"It is always sad when a member of a family passes from our midst . . ." Irene stands at the graveside looking expressionless, pale-lipped in the growing cold. On her left she holds Daniel's hand. He gazes curiously over the rim of the hole to the box beneath. Her right arm is supported by

Carol, who follows the boy's line of attention and regards the contents of the grave with undisguised contempt. ". . . how much greater must we feel the loss when the relative is taken from us prematurely." I stand directly across from Irene and could catch her attention were she not so preoccupied with assuming a blank stare. Peter is also here, as is Simon. Both find it difficult to know whether or not she registers their presence. She is the only reason anyone is here.

". . . and we can only be thankful that his restlessness is now at an end." It is a bravura performance, this vague obituary of a despised man. A casual passer-by could take away the impression that we were celebrating the departure of a modest man of modest means. The box is utilitarian and economic. And as to the scant mourners, who has more than six really good friends anyway?

I had collected Peter on my way to the service. Both of us passed Tom *en route*. They exchanged a look of frank embarrassment. I found restraint difficult.

"Aren't you going to ask us where we're going sober-suited in the middle of the day?"

"I know where you're going."

"Aren't you coming to join us?"

"No."

"Not even to celebrate the success of your little reprisal committee's handiwork?"

He levelled a stare at me without hostility.

"I'm glad the bastard is dead. And I'm not the only one. There must be about a dozen Orangemen at the lodge turning cartwheels. Don't try telling me you're going because you liked him."

"No, I'm not going to try telling you that."

Peter, embarrassed by the whole exchange, had walked on.

Elsbeth, on point of principle, refused to attend a papish service. She had tried to dissuade Simon from going. When she heard that both he and his employee intended going to the church she took the unprecedented step of staffing the Post Office herself for the period of their absence. This was not done out of any sense of loyalty to the Borough clientele.

There were not enough able-bodied men. We had to press-gang two of the mourners departing a previous service to take a rope each and lower McCullen to his resting place. Carol steered Irene away as soon as the coffin was out of sight. The gravel paths were hard underfoot in the cold. I crunched off after them with Simon and Peter.

"He'd be so soggy after a week in the Clyde," Peter said. "You'd think they'd be better burying him in a plastic bin bag rather than a box."

"Keep your voice down," I said. "Irene's just over there. And try not to seem so cheerful about the whole thing."

"As if she cares."

"Oh, she cares," Simon said. He had arrived late and alone after a final remonstrance with his wife. His small Ford was parked just beyond the cemetery gates. "I had intended that we could go back together, but," waving towards Irene her child and Carol, "if they've no other means of returning . . ."

"Do you suppose they brought McCullen here in a Transit?" Peter asked.

"Even if she came here in a hearse, she'd probably rather not return in one. We walked here and it's no hardship to walk back. Go and ask."

We saw him approach. The whole conversation was conducted through Carol. Irene kept her eyes on the ground and raised them only to give Simon a brief nod and a smile.

"She smiled at him," Peter said. "I bet he thought there was a fucking earthquake."

Elsbeth, sunning herself at the Post Office door in the slack mid-morning trade, watched the car pass and draw to a halt further down the street. She saw Simon emerge and deferentially hold the door ajar while helping Irene out. The distance was not so great to prevent her seeing the expression on his face. She returned indoors.

52

IN THE PAST THREE days Simon has become as aimless as the police investigation which has stultified in an air of heavy suspicion around Irene. The becoming wistfulness since my revelation in the pub has left him also. A stumbling interior logic has taken over and propelled him towards a conclusion.

It is night. He is climbing the steps towards Irene's flat with slow dread. She answers the doorbell. He is clutching flowers which he extends through the chink before the chain is removed. She starts back at the disembodied bunch before checking who is on the other side of the door. She says nothing, but smiles in embarrassed surprise and invites him in. He can hear Carol's voice from the lounge ahead talking into the hall, carrying on the conversation his entry interrupted. All the pegs on the coat rack are occupied. She tells him to leave his coat on the bed and walks back to join Carol. He has not been here since that night. As he lays his coat across the duvet he sees her splayed and bleeding. They are waiting for him in the lounge.

After a few minutes Irene gets up to make the inevitable tea and check on her sleeping children. Carol makes a few polite and uninterested enquiries of Elsbeth's health. She is avid to know the reason for his visit. When Irene returns the two women resume their conversation. He sits like a cigar-store Indian contributing nothing. The flow of talk finally slows and halts with his dampening presence. Carol takes her leave, Irene seeing her to the door. She departs with a questioning glance which is answered by a baffled shrug from the other woman.

Irene returns and clears up the tea things in the gathering silence. He summons himself to the point of clearing his throat just as she leaves the room. With uncharacteristic resolve he follows her through to the small kitchen. She can sense the imminence of some revelation and with alarm pre-empts him.

"If you want to make yourself useful put that away over there."

"Here?"

"No, th–"

"Oh, Christ! Sorry . . ."

He stoops over her bended form to help pick up the fragments and begins scouring the place for a dustpan, opening cupboards at random.

"Simon," it is the first time he can recall her using his name, "please don't slam the doors like that. The children are asleep just through the wall."

"Of course . . . I'm sorry." And after a pause, "the children, do they understand?"

It is a tactless transition. She stops over the broken pieces for a moment and replies without looking at him.

"You mean their father?"

"Yes."

"Elizabeth can't walk yet and Daniel seldom saw him when he wasn't drunk or recovering from drink. So the answer is no, they don't understand; and frankly, if they did, they probably wouldn't care."

"Yes. Still, it came as a blow to me – to us." Having spent his life dealing in circumspections he is surprised at his questions, even more at the directness of her replies.

"Did it?" She straightens. Her earlier affability has changed. At the mention of the children's father her voice has taken on an edge.

"Yes. Of course. There's no point in pretending. He wouldn't have won any popularity polls, but still . . ."

"Still what?"

"You know what they say about desperate diseases requiring desperate remedies."

She makes no reply but runs the water to begin washing the cups. He looks around making several redundant gestures.

"If you've a dish towel I'll dry."

"There's no need. They'll dry on the draining board."

"If you're sure." Again she makes no reply. He is unsure whether her manner is guarded or hostile. "I expect you're tired of receiving condolences."

"No. Not really. You're the first who's come out of their way to offer any. Everyone else skates round it."

"What about the police?"

"Yes. The police. I'm tired of the police."

"Haven't they offered their condolences?"

"Lots of times. Every time they ask me the same questions as last time, just to see if I give the same reply, they offer their condolences."

"I know it's none of my business, but I look on the whole thing as more of a reprieve than a tragedy." The line and delivery sound rehearsed because they are. The pretence of being preoccupied by the dishes is all used up. She sits down at the table with her face in her hands. He thinks she is crying and stands beside her, his hand hovering inches from the crown of her head, craving the contact he is afraid of making.

"Simon," the voice is thick and muffled, "what do you want?"

"They won't leave you alone, the police I mean, because you can't give them proof of where you were after . . . after . . ."

"After I was raped."

"Have you told them what – what happened?"

"Rape, Simon. The word is rape. You're the only one who saw the immediate after-effects and you can't even bring yourself to say the word. And you expect me to walk in and give physical evidence?" The rising cadence of her words alarm him. She has considered informing the police. The thought of intrusive investigations horrify her. She does not know how difficult it would be to obtain proof of violation so long after the event. It would be natural to ask why she did not come forward before. And a rape, substantiated or not, closely followed by the murder of the rapist would tend to corroborate their theories rather than her innocence.

"If they've no proof there's nothing they can do."

"I want to be left alone." She is sobbing through her hands.

"My wife was away that night, the night he raped you. If you say you were with me and I say you were with me, they'll have to leave you alone." Her stifled sobs slow and cease. He fetches her a wad of kitchen roll.

"Are you serious?"

"It's the first serious decision I've ever taken."

"And if I tell this to the police now, the first thing they'll ask is why I didn't tell them all this before and stop wasting all our times."

"Because I didn't give you permission before. You held this back so that I could salvage my marriage, but now that I've given this up as a lost cause I've told you to go ahead."

"You are serious."

"Yes."

"And what about your marriage?"

"I gave that up as a lost cause years ago when it got posted to Nairobi."

She can make nothing of the arcane remark besides the fact that the shyest man she knows stands before her prepared to perjure himself and ruin his reputation on the basis of their slight acquaintance.

"You and me, an illicit relationship?"

"Yes."

"I don't think they'd believe it."

"They don't have to believe it. They'll have two people prepared to swear where you were, and that wasn't where he was."

"Carol's already lied about my whereabouts on that night and got herself into trouble. I won't have you do it too."

He has foreseen this and is prepared with an alternative.

"There's another thing we can say."

"Why are you doing this?"

"McCullen hit me in public. You know about this?"

"Yes."

"I went for a walk that night. We met. We argued. He pulled out a knife like the one described in the papers last week. I disarmed him. We struggled. He fell . . ."

"This is pantomime. You disarmed him!"

"All right, I was carrying a knife."

"A kitchen knife?"

"Yes."

"Why would anyone go out at that time of night carrying a kitchen knife unless they intended to use it?"

"We can worry about that when they ask the question. The point is that he injured you in a way that you'd rather be suspected than tell what happened. And you've got no one who saw it happen. I've got two dozen people who saw him hit me. I had obvious reason."

"Why are you telling me this?" In her agitation she stands. He grips her wrists. "What do you want?"

"I've never done anything wrong. I could get a string of character witnesses. Your husband was a well-known lout. Lots of people saw him hit me. It's a factor in my favour. I lost my temper. I've no children and a wife who's got all the money out of me she wanted. And it's all she wanted. As far as either of us are prepared to make things public it'd be easier for me than for you." He stops. "Besides, it's not as if you'll do it again."

"You're mad!"

They look intently at one another. For an instant he sees them both, dispassionately, an attenuated point as his momentary vision widens: a middle-aged man and a young woman standing in an urban kitchen, framed in a lighted window among a myriad of such lights. He lets go her wrists. This time it is his turn to sit, dissipating what reserves remain with an uncontrollable shaking that rattles the glasses in the cupboard.

53

I HAVE RECEIVED my first letter from Audrey. It was dated on the eve of her return. It explains why she has not visited or called since getting back. It is brief, expressed with as much feeling as such news can be couched. Perhaps I misunderstood the "some artists" Katrine mentioned in passing. Perhaps this was a guarded hint which I was too obtuse to pick up on, to the other person who looks out between the lines of Audrey's letter. Perhaps there was some sisterly telepathy across the Atlantic, or a reticent admission over a telephone call. Perhaps she wanted the eloquence of her silence, or her sister's vague allusion, to convey the news I now read. So many perhaps.

By the timing of this I can see it is intended to pre-empt me from getting in touch with her, unknowing, and save the embarrassment of an interview.

Katrine came round and together we packed her things. Now that she's gone she's everywhere: in the circled numbers of my telephone directory; in the gaps of my bookshelves where my volumes lean diagonally; in the diamond of blood concealed on the underside of my upturned mattress, commemorating our improvident love-making. We filled empty boxes I filched from the supermarket, and plastic bags which I carried down laden like a Christmas tree. Then I went back to my empty flat.

Ruins are the most enduring form of architecture.

54

STUMBLING IN BRIGHT sunshine. Stumbling in a state akin to drunkenness that draws the curious attention of pedestrians. Stumbling past a vagrant woman, brushing on past the outstretched hands as the ferocious malediction follows in the wake. Thoughts crowding in, articulating themselves in the final summary: "That is the last voice I will hear, and it spoke to me in anger."

Stumbling up the stairs, clumsily manoeuvring the step ladder to the foot of the skylight. The precarious climb, encumbered with the necessary provisions. And other random thoughts: "Watch I don't fall backwards or I'll do myself a mischief." Metallic laughter as the irony registers. Fumbling the catch as the window swings ajar. Clambering on to the roof tiles heavily laden. The step ladder is drawn up behind, the skylight replaced to conceal evidence of the climb. It is a secluded eyrie, overlooking without being seen from adjacent roofs. It is a simple matter to buttress the ladder against the chimney stack without attracting attention and make for the top.

Straddling the apex, carelessly breaking slate tiles with a start of pain through the anaesthetic as the spine jars on the ridge. One leg is hoisted over in a sitting position. Balanced on the precarious rest, the bottle of mineral water is extracted from one pocket, a paper bag from another. The bag contains perhaps two dozen whole or partially broken pills and an inch of powder, the dust of those already pulped to fragments. The bottle is opened with difficulty and clamped between the knees, the bag arranged conically with touching thumb and forefinger ringing the neck. The raised bag filters a stream of powder to the open mouth. The process is ineffectual; a steady breeze distributes the stuff across the tiles. Coordination is also a problem: already an excessive dosage has numbed the faculties. Absorption into the bloodstream begins from the mouth. The lips and tongue have lost almost all sensation. What powder alights there is swallowed with difficulty. The bottle is raised, sluicing water down the throat to assuage a growing thirst. A continuous foam erupts from the corners of the mouth.

When the powder is finished the pills are attempted. These prove more difficult. Through the increasing drowsiness another expedient is hit upon. The bag is held firmly at the neck and beaten upon the tiles. One blow nearly causes a fall. A loose tile within arms' reach is prised loose and used as a blunt pestle. The resulting powder is poured into the half-empty bottle. One hand is placed over the top and the water is shaken into an opaque froth.

With great effort the bottle is raised to the lips and tilted, swallowing in deliberate mouthfuls as spillage slops over the cheeks and chin. The plastic slips from nerveless fingers, the bottle rolling down the angled roof to settle in the guttering. The air is cold and getting colder. In a last jolt of consciousness the faltering breath can be seen suspended in a plume against the grey slate. The eyes close, the body slumping forward, rolling down in the bottle's wake, progress arrested as the head cracks with full impetus against the chimney stack. A trickle of blood from the crown flows down the tiles to the waiting gutter. The body remains slumped, haemorrhaging quietly above a thoroughfare.

55

SIMON HAS TAKEN domestic incompetence to new heights. Twenty years of marriage and he cannot consummately fry an egg. Following his interview with Irene he sees himself for the first time to be thrown entirely on his own resources. He is determined to make a fist of it. In his new self-sufficiency he has gone as far as reintroducing to his bedroom whatever masculine paraphernalia takes his fancy, an easy step in Elsbeth's absence to her sister's. He has decided to cook. His modest repertoire is growing. He is improving from the early burnt offerings and incinerated meat. After a week of Elsbeth's absence he has produced something simple but edible: grilled lamb chops garnished with parsley, new potatoes and glazed carrots. Peter is the lucky recipient of these experiments. For the third time in a week he sits opposite Simon at the dinner table. A bottle of claret stands between them. They charge their glasses for the second time. Peter sniffs the air and licks his lips as if tasting the atmosphere. He has been doing this incessantly since his arrival.

"What's the matter?" Simon asks.

"Nothing. It's just . . ."

"Just what?"

"When did you buy these chops?"

"This evening. On my way home. After I left you."

"Do you think . . . Do you think they were quite fresh when they saw the grillpan?"

"There's still two uncooked in the fridge."

They sniff the plates before them. They take the uncooked chops from the fridge, unwrap them from their greaseproof paper and smell these also. Suspicions allayed they return to their meal and eat. The topic is forgotten and Simon sees his friend off at the door.

He sleeps uneasily, dreaming of unidentified animals burrowing through the ceiling above him, scratching their way through to attack his face. Next morning he is aware of the heavy smell of cooking which pervades the house from the previous night. He opens the upstairs windows before leaving for work, leaving all the inside doors ajar.

He is side-tracked to the bar on his way home and realises, with a pang of reproach, that he has been out on the past two occasions of Elsbeth's scheduled call. Out of principle he knows that she will not call at another time. He shrugs and orders another round. When he returns, pleasantly light-headed, the heavy smell of the morning still lingers. He notices with a disturbed curiosity that this is more noticeable upstairs where a through draught has been blowing all day.

The weekend rains consistently. Churchgoers emerge on Sunday afternoon to driving sleet as the temperature drops further. The smell has intensified. He imagines meat, putrefying behind the cooker where it has inadvertently been dropped. He and Peter begin a methodical search. They cover the kitchen meticulously. They search the remainder of the downstairs rooms. With no place left they go upstairs. The smell worsens. It has impregnated the curtains. Simon prepares for the worst and imagines some trapped cat.

It is Peter who notices the scraping from above which Simon has incorporated into his dream. They try to investigate but cannot find the stepladders. The rain has not slackened. There is a cascade of water outside the back window. Simon fears blocked guttering. Craning from the bathroom window with Simon sitting on the cistern holding his legs, Peter claims he can see something sticking above the gutter. Something cylindrical. Perhaps a bottle. They try to dislodge it with a bamboo cane till Peter asks to be hauled in, sopping wet from the falling sleet.

The following morning Simon makes two calls from the Post Office: one to Environmental Health in order that they can help him trace the smell to its source, one to the local handyman to clear the gutter. That afternoon the neighbours receive a gala performance.

The handyman ascends his ladder, dislodges and throws down the plastic bottle. Puzzled at the number of droppings which splatter the tiles, he climbs gingerly on to the roof, slipping on the excrement as he makes his way towards the chimney stack. Startled at his arrival, a cloud of dark crows flap heavily away, croaking their alarm. Whatever neighbours loiter at their windows during working hours can see him back out from behind the chimney. He loses his footing on the droppings and clutches wildly as he slides towards the edge. His foot gains purchase on the gutter, allowing him to edge towards the ladder. He descends rapidly, abandons his gear and walks down the hill towards the main street. His complexion is the opaque colour of the bottle he dislodged.

Ten minutes later a police car arrives. A uniformed constable makes the same careful climb. He does not descend but can be seen on the ridge of the roof, speaking into a radio, talking to his superior on the ground. In close sequence a fire engine and ambulance arrive. The presence of the three services attracts the curiosity of returning lunchtime schoolchildren, who loiter while their soup cools. Simon, ascending the hill with a baguette and a selection of cold meats under his arm, is nonplussed by the rank of flashing vehicles outside his door.

The neighbours see a hasty confabulation between Simon and the plainclothes man who appears to be directing operations. Two uniformed officers remove and collapse the handyman's ladder, carrying it inside as Simon opens the front door to a whole crowd of official people. He follows them, still clutching his groceries. A turntable ladder is also extended from the fire engine to the roof. Two ambulancemen carrying a collapsible stretcher climb up, followed by a supervising fireman and a police photographer. The skylight is thrown open as the crowd on the inside also make it to the roof, aided by the handyman's ladder. Congregating neighbours and onlookers who have come up from the Borough below discuss the possibility of a cave-in with the weight exerted on the rooftiles by the biomass. Circling crows continue to caw angrily, circling above the sombre crowd huddled around their interrupted meal. For the third time Simon attempts to climb through the open skylight and is denied access by a polite constable whose bulk occupies the whole strip of sky.

The sky clouds again with the threat of rain. The crowd below persevere through the first drops and are rewarded by irregular flashes from the rooftop as the police photographer carries out his macabre task. The ambulancemen struggle down with a loaded stretcher, followed by the complete retinue as the rain starts, dispersing onlookers and drumming on the multitude of smashed tiles on Simon's ruined roof.

He accompanies the cortège down to the Borough. A solitary constable left in possession of his house and his lunch cheerfully slices the baguette as the cars disappear. Another unmarked police car rounds the corner and screeches to a dramatic halt outside the house. A row of lace curtains across the way are lifted again in genteel curiosity. The two men who have questioned everyone regarding McCullen's death emerge, rush up and beat a tattoo on Simon's front door. Their movements are dynamic even if their investigation is dead. The constable answers, happily munching, interrupting his meal for a leisurely explanation at the door. He concludes by pointing in the direction the cars have gone. Dejected they return to their car and drive slowly downhill.

56

TO SAVE HIM THE grief I stood in for Simon as one of the family. What family? She was identified by my grim nod and the high-class orthodontics she'd had carried out in an expensive surgery uptown. I talked to the pathologist, the same who had examined McCullen. He told me her week on the roof had left her worse for wear than McCullen's week in the Clyde.

When they straightened her body out they found a large sheaf of sodden letters clasped to her chest. Those on the outside had been soaked. Once they read a few of the remainder it wasn't difficult to guess the contents of those letters the rain had spoiled. All were addressed to her sister. Simon found another drawerful in her bureau. The earliest dated from almost ten years ago, the latest, carried with her to the roof, were written in erratic script on what must have been the eve of her suicide. Periods between were not uniform. Sometimes months passed between correspondence; in one case a year was allowed to elapse. She had been prolific of late. In the past four months she'd dashed off one, sometimes even two, letters in a single day. It was a calendar of growing derangement.

To all purposes it might have been one letter written over years with months between paragraphs. It consisted of a continuous tirade on every conceivable aspect of the people with whom she came in contact. She ranted at Simon, his employees, her neighbours, her fellow churchgoers, casual acquaintances, her dead parents, her own sister to whom the letters were addressed and never sent. She enjoyed the licence of outrage. Carol was a "whore", Irene a "sanctimonious whore". Simon was nothing; his insignificance filled bitter pages. Her feelings towards McCullen and elaboration of what had happened were unequivocal. A lifetime of vitriol was given expression in unsent letters, carried at the last beside her corroded heart. The sight of that bundle, the bitter digest of such a life, was worse than the mutilated woman they found in a half-crouch at the chimney stack. I wasn't struck at the gore. I've seen worse. I left thinking what a waste.

At least they'd leave Irene alone.

57

I STOOD ON ONE side of Simon, Peter on the other, mirroring the arrangement of Irene and her companions two weeks previously. It had been a bright day with a bitter hoar frost that never lifted. The narrow ditch must have been gouged out. Sods piled beside the hole had frozen into blocks of masonry. Despite the cold they turned out in their scores. There was a huge Catholic contingent there too, testifying more to the esteem in which Simon was held than to any fond memories of Elsbeth.

They had fitted us in at short notice. The service had been scheduled for the early afternoon. It was a deep winter of early twilights and the night cold had come in to settle before the sunlight was on the wane. I looked round the circle of faces and to the heads beyond receding down the hill, bodies turning the colour of gingerbread as the premature dark stole on us. Plumes of the breathing crowd rose and I could hear them shuffle, deferentially restraining from stamping their freezing feet. And Simon stood between us, oblivious to the silent tribute, totally bewildered and reproachful at his numbed lack of grief.

As we dispersed I excused myself for a moment and threaded my way through the crowd to overtake Irene, whom I had glimpsed standing at the back. I touched her shoulder with my gloved hand.

"Thank you for coming."

She stood still for a moment not knowing what to say as the people brushed past us.

"I hear you and Peter have moved in with him."

"No. Not really. Not really moved in. We're just there, taking it in shifts. Just till he gets on his feet, as it were."

"Yes."

"We can just as easily move out again."

"What's that supposed to mean?"

I let her go on and went back upstream to find my friends.

58

CHRISTMAS HAS COME and gone like a succession of Sundays with closed shops and uneventful days. The weather has remained stubbornly unemblematic. The same sombre air doesn't prevail over the whole Borough. At night I can hear the usual rioters and their muted songs ring hollowly up the frozen streets. Three days after Christmas there was a light snowfall in the early evening. We were left with a crisp mantle that changed the complexion of the place in fifty minutes. I'd been warming my feet at Simon's hearth with the other two, picking my way through the endless chicken when Peter saw the snow and ran to the window like a child. We both walked out in the soft hiss with Simon watching from the lounge. Peter began making snowballs and thudding them into the window that separated us.

"You'll break it."

"So fucking what? It's like a museum in there. All we need's Elsbeth stuffed in a glass case, like that tiger. Know the one I mean?"

"Yes."

"Let's have a party."

"What?"

"It'd be good for him."

"I think you had better ask."

"You know he'd say no. He's miserable because he's looked inside and knows he's not sad. Not really sad. He'd say it's too soon after the funeral. He's never had a party in his life. It'd be the best present we could give. The air in that place hasn't moved for years. Let's fill up his house with drunk people. Let's get lots of men and lots of women and lots and lots of drink and let's not tell him till it's too late."

There was an ebullient logic to this and his enthusiasm was contagious. He knew he'd won when I didn't object quickly enough. Without a coat and still in slippers he ran shrieking across Simon's lawn and down towards the Borough. He'd have no trouble recruiting in the dog days between Christmas and Hogmanay. I fetched my jacket and cheque book, fobbed off Simon's enquiries and trudged off towards the supermarket, borrowing one of their trolleys for the return trip. I bought three slabs of beer and some cheap wine and two types of Pimms and some fruit and some other things for making punch. My credit wouldn't stretch any further. On my way back I met Peter with two friends I barely knew, Carol with her latest beau and Ivan ready for a bottle of brown sauce. Peter sat in the trolley as we pushed it up the hill. The promised cohorts, they said, were arriving in due course. Each of them had thoughtfully provided themselves with drink.

They invaded the hall and Simon took their coats with a look of alarm. Two immediately telephoned friends to tell them of the venue. There are more drifting partygoers at that time of year in the Borough than there are parties. "Call Irene," I said to Carol.

We sat in that empty house, eight of us trying to kid on we were a crowd till they started to arrive in droves. I don't know what the average age was that night. Nearer Peter's than Simon's. Within ten minutes the house pulsed with noise and some music imported for the occasion. I called Irene and tried to tempt her out. I could barely make myself heard above the mayhem. Simon tried forty minutes of being host, taking the coats of people he had never seen before and would probably never see again, dispensing drinks, cradling an ashtray until he gave it up as a bad job. Some people carelessly rubbed out cigarettes on the parquet floor in a way that would have apoplexed Elsbeth. He saw and I noticed him make his way through the crowded lounge with a damp cloth. I saw Peter also, deliberately heading to intercept. He caught hold of Simon's arm extending towards the stain.

"What the fuck," he said, "she's dead. Let her go."

It was the only capricious thing I saw him do which showed any intelligence. If he hadn't been drunk he wouldn't have been brave or foolhardy enough to have said it. I saw Simon recoil in conventional horror and then consider for a moment. He knew it was well intentioned and came from someone who loved him more than his wife ever had. A slow smile spread across his face in the course of the exorcism. He nodded to us both and turned towards the kitchen still holding the dripping cloth.

"Throw the fucking thing out!" Peter shouted, yanking the front door open. People turned at the freezing draught. With an ill-practised lob Simon limply hit the doorjamb. I kicked it out into the night and slammed the door behind. I walked up to Simon.

"It's gone to Nairobi, to join Elsbeth." He nodded. "You're not sad now?"

"No." Peter approached and threw his arms round us both in drunken *bonhomie*.

"Get the fucking beers in," he said. Simon smiled, disengaged himself and went to fetch the drink.

"I think it's going to be all right," Peter said. And then again, when I didn't reply, "I said, I think it's going to be all right."

"Yes," I said.

Was it for this I came?

59

THERE ARE MANY THINGS I cannot do. Do not expect
of me the talents demonstrated by my spurious predecessors in popular culture. I cannot dictate appropriate little
homilies on vacant typewriters, or imbue some unfortunate
with a love of life by showing them the consequences of
their non-existence. If I had the gift of investing things with
meaning I would not be here.

I have always had a great sympathy with Cathy, who
dreamed she was in heaven, Heathcliffless, and broke her
heart with weeping to return. And she was flung out into
the middle of the heath by the legions, angered by her
ingratitude, and woke up sobbing for joy.

I appear to be defined by things I cannot do. I am laden
with negative potentialities. I have dreams of a fortunate
reprieve: to wake in gratuitous happiness, surprised by joy.

60

SINCE THE NOVELTY of that unprecedented night,
Simon has thrown open house to the Borough for two days.
He has been the prodigal father, lavish with his dead wife's
provisions. His cupboards are empty. Surfeited with this
new-found hospitality, given vent in Elsbeth's absence, he
moves among the wreckage happily clearing up. Peter and
I have remained to help. Tomorrow is Hogmanay, a por-
tentous midnight. Preparations are under way all over the

city. At the height of the festivities during Simon's party, Peter mounted the half-landing and tried to address everyone. Unable to make himself heard above the noise, he had one of his cronies turn the music down.

"Tomorrow," he shouted, "tomorrow night is Hogmanay . . ."

"Tomorrow night is two nights from Hogmanay," someone corrected.

"Details . . ." with a dismissive wave. "Hogmanay they're having fireworks all over the city to ring out the old year and ring in the new. Fireworks. Well we've enjoyed enough hospitality here already . . ." I thought that was rich. He'd invited everyone here either himself or by proxy. He went off at a drunken tangent and ranted about Simon's generosity. Several people charged their glasses and bestowed indiscriminate smiles all round, obviously having no idea whose hospitality they were enjoying.

"The fireworks," I reminded. The party was quickly stagnating without the narcotic beat so many of them seemed to need.

"Across the city!" he shouted again. The milling thoughts were having trouble getting to his mouth now. "Best place to see them's probably the Queen's Park flagpole on the South Side. We can go there. We can all go there."

He stopped shouting abruptly and sat down. The performance was received with a cheer and the music started almost immediately. It was difficult to tell how well the suggestion had gone down. If as many people as this wanted to congregate again, no one else of our acquaintance had a house big enough to accommodate them. Simon's sense of generosity might have taken a battering after a binge like this. Guests and fish, like the man says, stink after three days. The venue was ideal. Again, inadvertently, Peter had hit upon a good idea.

"That's twice in one night you've said something sensible," I told him. "There's hope yet."

I stopped drinking in the early hours. Irene didn't show at all despite my efforts. People began to leave in desultory groups, the remainder to pair off, retiring to the furniture earlier pushed out of the way to make room for the dancing. Peter sat on the edge of an armchair replenishing his glass from a bottle on the side table, talking to Simon who sat in exhausted content, half listening. In the dim light I picked my way between the recumbent couples, picking up half-empty glasses and the cans used as ash trays with a residue of beer and tumid fag ends. A scum of pulped fruit was all that remained of the punch. I found a vacant bed upstairs and fell into a dreamless sleep.

We spent a day and part of the next cleaning up the aftermath. We were all three glad to be going to the South Side for the New Year fireworks; glad of one another's company and a temporary break from it; glad of a night of cold outdoors after petrifying in Elsbeth's mausoleum.

Early Hogmanay and the Borough seemed to be littered with itinerant partygoers flitting from one gathering to the next. As I walked down the hill following the other two I could hear the noise spill out from the pubs which lined the main road. Jaded as we were all three felt galvanised at history raging around as the Borough and the city hummed in preparation for the new decade. There were women at ten o'clock at night cleaning their doorsteps and sluicing out the closes lest the new year find them grimy, as if establishing the standard, wiping the slate. Through the windows I could see children, bathed, dressed in Sunday finery and allowed up to unaccustomed hours to hear in the bells. There were flowers put at lighted windows. I began to feel it then, multitudinous and vibrant as I walked down the hill into the noise and the light.

They were three-deep at the bar and the clamour hit me as soon as I opened the door. The place was ringed with Victorian mirrors bearing the logotype of the brewery, reflecting the light and the faces. Shouted conversations were conducted across a dozen others. There were several greetings as we entered. Simon ordered us two beers and himself an orange juice. I said I would drive and gave him a last opportunity. He declined.

We stayed till about half past ten. Almost everyone came through at one point, accepting the general invitation to Queen's Park provided they could find transport. It was rumoured that the buses were running late and free. Several people had offered to drive. I could pick them out, marked by their sobriety as we spilled into the street. We comprised a motley group. There was a small cavalcade of cars by the time we were ready to leave, pumping horns in exuberance. A drunkard I had never seen attempted to get into Simon's car carrying his dog. "It's a firework display," I explained. It didn't seem to register. "The dog will be terrified." He accepted this and stumbled off into the night. We were around the last to leave. A plump lady whose sister was in the car in front occupied most of the back seat with Peter. We were pulling away from the kerb when I saw Irene run towards us carrying Daniel. In the glare of the headlights she didn't recognise who the driver was. When we drew up alongside at her wave, she shielded her eyes, glanced inside and stood back in embarrassment.

"I got a sitter for Elizabeth," she explained, panting. "It's just that – well, the boy. I'd like him to see the fireworks. He might not get the chance again . . ."

"Not in a thousand years," I said, clambering out. It was a two-door. I pushed the seat forward and squeezed into the back. She had no alternative but to get in. I reached forward and took Daniel to sit on my lap. When she climbed into the front she had a deep blush that I could see in the dark, mirroring Simon's.

We drove to the South Side for the most part in utter silence. The plump woman had a few attempts at civility which drew a blank in the tension of the small car. I reached between the front seats and turned on the radio. A broad-casted party anticipated the bells with forced jollity. It sounded a gross collage of things remotely Scottish. I turned it off. As we crossed the Clyde I could see the globes of light from the suspension bridge reflected in the still water. When we reached the park the fat lady muttered a hurried thanks and bustled off to find her sister, obviously pleased to be rid of us. I heard her say she'd had better fun watching the electricity meter.

Others besides our group had obviously had the same idea. A large crowd from all over the city had assembled outside the main gates. As we approached we met a trickle of people turning away, mentioning to us in passing that the gates were closed and entry forbidden on the grounds of safety. Sure enough, a padlock and chain had been fastened round the central stanchions, descending bolts driven home into the ground below. People milled around pur-poselessly. At night the park is full of truant children who squeeze past gaps in the fence. Peter found one and pushed himself through. Several others did likewise. In moments everyone was looking for a convenient hole. I saw the plump lady and her equally plump sister, too fat to trespass, walk along the perimeter fence looking for an opening big enough.

"It's called a gate," Peter said.

Once inside and away from the road it was like pitch. We dispersed into random groups in the dark, making ragged progress towards the flagpole. As much in gratitude for the lift, or perhaps because she could not recognise another familiar face in the gloom, Irene remained with us. We were under a canopy of trees which stretched up in an avenue towards our destination. The sky above was bright. The weathermen had predicted a clear moon. It would get lighter when we cleared the foliage.

There were other figures making their way slowly through the dark. Still smarting from his encounter with the police, Peter kept nervously dragging us aside.

"It's the parky!" he hissed.

"If it is there must be a gang of them, and one's only two feet tall."

A family brushed past. A woman with the same idea as Irene had brought her son. The mothers exchanged a brief pleasantry, the remarks incongruous in our surroundings. Simon hauled Peter out of a bush and we continued.

The trees thinned nearer the top of the hill, which flattened at the summit in an artificial circular plateau. The flagpole stood in the centre of this. A picket fence ringed the perimeter, which was properly policed. But there were too many people now arrived for the park-keepers to evict, besides which, everyone could see the assembled crowd were predisposed to having a good time: there would be no trouble. A stretch of grass beneath the plateau sloped in a downward curve towards the main gates, towards the city centre, the direction in which the fireworks would be launched. The crowd gathered here. As we cleared the trees and approached, the moon came out. I could see there must have been literally hundreds of people flapping their arms in the cold and crunching from foot to foot in the brittle snow. There were sporadic bursts of singing too and lots of people proffering cans and bottles. The sight gladdened me. Daniel was straining at his mother's arm.

"Let him go," Peter said.

"Keep close," she ordered. As soon as she let go he ran towards the people. Already I could see several faces I knew.

We found the Borough group. I had lost all track of time. The park-keepers, who had lit a fire of deadwood to keep themselves warm, allowed us to congregate round. They also shared in the distributed cans. Simon had taken charge of Daniel near the fire. I saw Irene look anxiously across.

"He'll be all right," Peter said. Carol was there without the man who had escorted her to Simon's party.

"You're such an expert with other people's kids," she said. Irene left the child with Simon.

I began to feel a curious sense of complete detachment. The breathing people, the glowing cigarette ends, the ascending sparks, the occasional glint from the muddied snow. I made a few halting replies to the good-humoured remarks. I had some trouble getting the words out. No one appeared to notice.

I look around. Carol is talking to Peter, conducting what looks like an amiable argument. They appear to be leaning towards one another, prefiguring something. There is an intimacy in their shared preoccupation. Irene is with her son who is with Simon. She is standing some feet away watching them both. Looking at all five I think there is a preposterous and beautiful equation here.

I walk up to Irene and stand before her with my back to Simon and Daniel. "You can't hector someone into loving you." She looks at me levelly. We understand one another.

"If you can't find it in yourself to love him, you can't stop him from loving you."

"I know that."

"If you can't love him at least be good to him."

She says nothing but takes my hand between both of hers and squeezes it hard. Having made my bungling prescription I feel suddenly embarrassed and redundant.

"Excuse me," I hear myself say.

A hush falls. People are checking their watches. A spontaneous cheer breaks upon the outrolling of the first slow toll, interrupted in its turn by the fusillade which breaks out from behind and above us as the first rockets hiss over our heads towards the city, bursting in bright flares. From the People's Palace on Glasgow Green they are being launched simultaneously, and from Victoria Park, and from the East End, and half a dozen places, the sky suddenly erupting in a canopy of white light. I look around at us all, thrown into momentary relief.

The colours start, the first explosion a dazzling green which falls in tendrils, each exploding in their turn. I want Audrey to see this. Perhaps she does. Irene has picked up Daniel and he is reaching up to the sky, clutching at the splendour. They are launching red rockets from the People's Palace and another fusillade from behind us turns cobalt. There are jubilant shouts among the deafening cracks and bangs. Another rocket swerves in a faulty trajectory into the tangle of overhead branches, hissing till it liberates itself in a shower of sparks, arcing up into the night. I think of the child's balloon on my way to Audrey. Where is she now? Of whom is she thinking? I see her, sitting in silence with her coiled thoughts, long-limbed, sweetly cleft.

I look at them all, shouting and pointing in excitement.

There are others I have not introduced: Elaine, ill-equipped for the cold with her absurdly short skirt, cotton top and exposed neck; Alasdair, with whom I vie to lend her a scarf; Kenneth and Mary, inseparable, she stiff-lipped and English, he stiflingly uxorious with his unmarried wife. And the others. And suddenly I feel an immense pity for them and a hope that they will be spared. Spared the small desolations and the conflagrations of the heart. All of them. Those I know and those I do not. And the unworthy.

Bursting over the park and the people and the buildings and the river. Bursting over the houses and the Borough. Bursting over the churches and the dance halls and the cinemas and the brothels. Bursting and bursting and bursting.

My heart is bursting.

The rockets are less frequent now. I can see the burning embers fall into vapour. There is the sharp tang of gunpowder. Smoke from the fire has risen to meet the descending pall. Again the sporadic singing starts, the inevitable "Auld lang syne". I can barely see the spires of the adjacent churches, the cloud-capp'd towers.

Should auld acquaintance be forgot.

And never brought to mind.

The buildings are melting into the air. Into thin air. So are the people. I can barely see my friends. They are becoming insubstantial. Their singing is fainter and fainter.

It is the millennium. My millennium. It is not they who are leaving. I am. I wish them well under the night. It is my reprieve. What else is there for a superannuated angel?

It was for this I came.